# Between Two Worlds

by **Sandra Brand**

*For Michael
best wishes
Sandra Br'any
March 1991*

SHENGOLD PUBLISHERS, INC.

New York City

ISBN 0-88400-083-4 [Hardcover]
ISBN 0-88400-084-2 [Paperback]
Library of Congress Catalog Card Number: 82-60204
Copyright © 1982 by Sandra Brand

All rights reserved

Published by Shengold Publishers, Inc.
23 W. 45th St., New York, N.Y. 10036

Printed in the United States of America

# Between Two Worlds

# 1

*God creates new worlds constantly—
by causing marriages to take place.*

Zohar

The marriage took place in the house of a poverty-stricken rabbi who, for twenty-five zlotys, agreed to perform the ceremony without the parental permit required for minors, as I was under eighteen. His one-room apartment was crowded with ancient cabinets, bookcases, scratched tables, and broken chairs pushed back against the peeling walls. The place had the appearance of a warehouse except that in the center of the room stood a canopy.

There were two witnesses. In addition, the rabbi had supplied a quorum of ten men from among his friends to recite the prayers. Neither Mark's parents nor mine were present since we had eloped.

Standing under the canopy I tried to concentrate upon the meaning of the ceremony, but found myself distracted by a ridiculously unimportant detail. The rabbi's wife had insisted upon covering my head with a scarf. It might have been pink at one time; now it was faded. I had not looked in the mirror after she placed her scarf on my head to serve as a sort of veil, but I knew that I looked awkward and felt embarrassed each time Mark looked my way. My discomfort increased when I noticed the expression of annoyance on Mark's face as he was led by the rabbi to circle around me seven times in the Orthodox tradition.

After he had shattered the glass by stamping on it, we were pronounced man and wife. Mark kissed me lightly and rushed me out of the rabbi's place, away from the poor neighborhood of Place Teodora toward Valy Hetmanskie and Legionov leading to Akademicka, a better section of Lvov. My arm linked in his, I walked beside him proud of my new status as a married woman and watched the fine snowflakes melt as fast as they fell on his coat.

"We have an early winter this year," I said to break the silence. And after a while I asked, "Will you miss me?"

He turned to me and his glance through his eyeglasses embraced me warmly. "What a silly question. I'll wait for next October just like you, Roma. And I'll mark off each day on the calendar until our separation is over."

I moved closer to him and whispered: "A year is a long time."

He pressed my arm gently and said: "I understand how you feel, but, Darling, this is the only way."

I clung to him until we entered the Bristol Restaurant. The waiter asked Mark what he wished to order for his daughter and himself.

I pretended not to have heard.

During the meal Mark sat across from me; he didn't reach out to touch my hand once. Was he dismayed by the waiter's remark referring to me as his daughter? Was it my fault that at eighteen I looked younger and he older at thirty-six? Suspended in silence, interrupted by remarks about the tenderness of the *Wiener Schnitzel*, Mark sighed. I wondered why.

We had to hurry to my cousin Gina's, on Leone Sapiehy, to collect Mark's luggage to be in time for the two o'clock train. Gina greeted me with a curious stare. We had been roommates during high school days, and had promised never to keep secrets from one another. While Mark was busy with his luggage, she took me aside and whispered: "You shouldn't let your husband go away like this. He will soon forget you."

"Forget me? We are married now, and what's more important, we are in love."

"You don't know men. Out of sight, out of mind. You should spend some time with him before you let him go."

"But his employer kept him in Niemirov the two days we

had planned to spend in Lvov. He must leave for his new job or lose it."

"Didn't you say he would have to change trains in Komarov? Why not stay overnight in Komarov? You can take the morning train back to Lvov and he can go on to Cracow."

# 2

*Love turns one person into two;
and two into one.*

*Immanuel of Rome, Machbaroth*

Mark readily accepted my suggestion to accompany him and we arrived in Komarov that same evening.

The only conveyance available from the railroad station to the town was an open wagon pulled by two decrepit horses. The seats for six passengers consisted of wooden boards covered with straw, with nothing to support our backs and nothing to hold on to when the wagon slid or bumped over the snow-covered cobbled streets.

My fur-lined coat kept me warm for only the first few minutes. I pushed my cold hand into Mark's, but his lack of response caused me to withdraw it. Disappointed, I saw in the fading light his finely shaped nose, red from the cold. Soon, I thought, my own would be in the same state. Another sideward glance revealed his profile and his English mustache covered with frost. For a moment he put his arm protectively around my shoulder but took it away instantly.

We were discharged at the Market Place which was crowded with similar vehicles. They belonged to peasants who had brought their produce into town to sell or barter for such items as salt, kerosene, saccharine—the latter preferred since it was cheaper than sugar—and other items that the farmer could not himself supply.

Their women stopped in textile shops to buy gaily colored kerchiefs while the husbands enjoyed the leisure of a few drinks at the local bars and more comfortably concluded those larger deals begun earlier in the bitter cold of the Market Place.

While Mark paid the driver, I stamped my feet against the hard packed snow to bring back the circulation. Mark stopped a police officer, and his inquiry as to where we could find a clean hotel sounded crude to me, as if he were shouting our intentions to the world which should have remained only between ourselves.

The officer looked at me curiously, opened his mouth to say something, but instead merely pointed across the Market Place to a street, shaking his head as we turned away.

The hotel, like most in small towns of Poland, consisted of several rooms, all of them on the ground floor. The air in the front room which served as a bar was thick with Machorka (a cheap tobacco) smoke, although only a few peasants lingered at scattered tables drinking their final vodkas before returning to their own villages.

When the stocky proprietress, wearing a bandana, opened the glass paneled door, mentioning that this was the only room available in her establishment, I paused for a moment at the doorway before I entered. During the four-hour ride in the train with Mark, leaning against him, I had been longing for night and for just such a room, any room where we could be alone. Now, seeing its twin beds separated only by a night table, I dreaded the thought of being alone with a stranger.

The room, clean, cold, was divided by a thin partition from the other rooms. The proprietress standing in the open door, her tremendous bosom protruding, gave me a brief, searching glance.

By now I had become accustomed to being stared at with curiosity when accompanied by Mark.

She wanted to speak to him but he took no notice. He was busy wiping his gold-rimmed glasses. Had he chanced to look up, his short-sighted vision would not have taken in the scene.

"If you don't want to be disturbed," the proprietress said, "you'd better lock yourselves in. It's impossible for me to control our vodka drinking guests at all times."

Mark quickly adjusted his glasses so that he could watch closely as she demonstrated the way to secure the door from the inside. She drew the white curtains with a flourish, and then left us alone.

I bent down to remove my snowshoes. When I straightened up, Mark had already rid himself of his jacket, sweater, tie and shirt. He tossed everything on the same chair while I stood undecided, holding both shoes in one hand, wondering where to put them so as not to mess up the immaculately clean floor.

Mark, sitting on one of the beds facing me, beckoned to me as I stood rooted unable to move, wishing he would fetch me and carry me to bed.

He did no such thing.

He beckoned to me again, this time with a wider gesture.

I went toward him, slowly, and stopped between the two beds, my snowshoes still in my hand.

He rose, took the shoes from me and flung them out of the way. They hit the floor with a thud.

He pulled me down, showered me with short kisses, scattered them over my face and teased my skin with his mustache, not yet dry from the frost. He began to unbutton my cardigan, then the blouse beneath. I trembled. "Are you still cold?" he asked in a whisper.

He had to repeat the question before I answered. "Only my feet," I said.

He disentangled himself from the embrace, knelt on the floor and started to massage my feet.

I didn't like him stooping before me and drew him up. When his chest, covered with fine brown hair, pressed against my breasts, I was beginning to grow dizzy and wanted time to stand still.

Mark was now kneeling on the bed. As he was peeling off the rest of his clothing I was suspended in expectation. There was a knock on the door. Suddenly all this pleasure was gone, and I felt a void because Mark had jumped to his feet. "Who's there?" he called.

"It's me, the proprietress. I brought a hot-water bottle for your wife. The poor child looked half frozen."

I had hoped after marrying a man of thirty-six never to be called a child again. But here it was. She knew I was a married woman and still referred to me as a child.

Mark opened the door a little, took the bottle from the proprietress and placed it under the huge feather-quilt. He looked at me with laughing eyes and asked: "Will you let me share it with you?"

"Of course. 'For better or for worse, till death do us part.'"

He switched off the light and I thought with relief how much easier it would be for me to respond to his caresses. I heard him coming barefoot toward me.

"Why didn't you undress as I asked you? We're husband and wife now!"

He started exactly where he had left off when the proprietress had interrupted, pulling at my skirt. Something ripped—and he stopped abruptly. "You'd better do it yourself," he said.

I wanted to obey him, but I couldn't move. No, I could not undress myself. No, I could not appear to be wanting him. But when I heard his annoyed voice in the dark, "What's the matter with you!" I quickly undressed. Naked, I lay back tensely waiting.

The moment he embraced me I wanted very much to sustain the unity created by that embrace and for a moment he did remain still, as if in response to my silent wish. Then I was embarrassed for having shown desire for the nearness of his body. "A woman doesn't give herself, a woman surrenders," I had been told by my close girl friends, but soon I forgot the advice of my girl friends, of my parents, and of the book I had read, lost in the joy experienced for the first time.

The impact of the new pleasure was overwhelming.

As if mutilated into a thousand pieces, yet all connected by the center of me, I smiled happily as he supported himself on his elbow and looked at me more lovingly than ever before. Gently he brushed a strand of hair from my forehead and eased down to the pillows. I turned to one side, curled up against the living warmth, felt his arm around me and safely drifted into nothingness.

# 3

*Without ethical culture there
is no deliverance for mankind.*

*Albert Einstein*

Did I hear a knock?
It took several moments to collect my senses. Yes, somebody was banging away at the door.

Slowly, Mark loosened his grip on me. He groaned, stretched himself, and finally said: "Who can it be, who the hell can that be?" He rolled off the bed, switched on the light, and called out: "Who is it? Can't a man have privacy in his own room?"

Hoarse laughter sounded from behind the locked door followed by a loud order, "Open Up!"

Mark called back "I'm not opening up until I know who's there." Naked, holding his glasses in his hand, his shortsighted eyes burning with anger, Mark crossed the room from corner to corner, "Did you see my bathrobe?" he asked for the third time.

"Why don't you look in your suitcase?"

He rummaged in his suitcase, found his robe, slipped into it, then went to the door. Passing a mirror, he stopped to brush his hair, all the while the voice outside was becoming shriller and more demanding.

"Open the door in the name of the law! It's the police! Open the door or I'll break it open!"

Mark opened the door.

I pulled the feather-quilt up to my chin.

The same policeman who had directed us to the hotel staggered in, drunk. "Both of you show me your papers," he ordered.

Mark began to search for his trousers which he had discarded in such haste. He found them on the floor near the chair with the rest of his clothes. He went through every pocket, found his wallet, emptied the contents and said: "You'll pay for this, you'll pay. It's illegal what you're doing. You'll pay for it. I'm an attorney. Did you know I'm an attorney?"

"So you're a lawyer, ha?" the policeman said. "All lawyers are shit to me." Swaying on his feet he reached for the bar membership card Mark had found. He carried the card closer to the light and read the print with difficulty. He looked hard at the photograph and fixed his inflamed eyes on Mark's face. "That's him, all right," he reassured himself and turning to me, he said: "*Your* identification papers!"

"She doesn't need any," Mark said quickly. "She's my wife. I'm an attorney and she's my wife. For Christ's sake, can't you see that you're making a mistake? It may cost you your job!"

"Look who's threatening me. A lawyer for all I know. I'm afraid of no one, least of all Jewish lawyers."

Though my papers still carried my maiden name—since we were married only in a religious ceremony—I asked Mark to bring my pocketbook from the dresser.

The policeman came close to the bed, took my papers, compared them with Mark's and said triumphantly: "I knew it, I knew it from the first moment I laid eyes on you two that something was fishy. Here it is in black and white. Who ever heard of a husband and wife having different names, ha? You're *not* husband and wife."

"I swear we are," I said.

"Both of you come along."

"I have a colleague here in town. I should like to see him first," Mark said and started to dress.

"Who do you want to see, Kaminski or Linzer?"

"I want to see Dr. Linzer."

"All right, you can see him. But I'm coming along so you can't sneak out of town," the policeman said as he shuffled Mark out of the room.

As soon as the door closed behind them, I leaped out of bed, opened my overnight bag and took out the blue nightgown Gina had so carefully selected for me. It was made of fine, hand-embroidered silk and, as I donned it, I noticed that it exposed every curve of my body; the style of it made my breasts appear larger than they really were.

Mark will like it, I thought, standing before the mirror which also reflected my flushed face. Will I ever overcome the habit of blushing, I wondered.

Back in bed, I curled up under the quilt and maneuvered the still warm hot-water bottle between my feet. Poor Mark, out in the cold while I was comfortable in bed. Wasn't it all my fault? It was I who appeared to be too young to be married, too young to be the wife of such a mature man, too young to be away from home and parents. And I was the one who had suggested a night in Komarov. It was all my fault. I hoped that his colleague would be able to resolve this matter, but what if he couldn't?

I wished I were home, safe with my parents, with Mark and all the ensuing complications gone like a frightening dream. Then I rejected these thoughts and gently brushed my hand over the pillow Mark's head would once again rest on after his return.

The proprietress, her hands buried in the pockets of her red-blue-black striped apron, entered through the now unlocked door. She apologized for the incident claiming that the policeman was no less drunk today than he had been every market day. "He'd do better watching his own daughter," she said. "She's only fifteen and already a tramp."

"What takes them so long? My husband should be back by now." The use of the word "husband" for the first time sounded unnatural to my ears. I could only hope that the same word didn't sound as strange to the proprietress.

"It takes time. Maybe Dr. Linzer was already in bed and had to get dressed. You never can tell, can you? Poor little girl." She took one hand out of her pocket, adjusted her bandana and touched my shoulder.

I wanted to rebuke her for presuming to call me child and little girl, but the sympathy in her voice and the warmth of her calloused hand on my shoulder made my anger evaporate. As tears came to my eyes, tears came to her eyes, and I knew she believed me and was on my side. I grasped her hand and confided the reason for my secret wedding.

"Mark came to my hometown two months ago. We live in Niemirov—"

"I know Niemirov, it's famous for the sulphur and mud baths."

"He came to Niemirov for two months to replace one of our two attorneys who planned to go for a vacation. When his time was up, both of us knew we were madly in love and decided to get married. But, his sister, ten years older, was set against this marriage—"

"Why? You seem to be a nice girl and you're pretty too—"

"She had worked hard to help Mark through three degrees in various colleges and had expected some kind of repayment. Her hope that her younger brother would marry into wealth, or get at least an eight-thousand dollar dowry would be dashed if Mark married me—"

"Why?"

"Because my parents, having three daughters, can only afford three thousand dollars and everybody knows that with such a dowry a matchmaker would introduce a girl to a clerk, not a lawyer. And besides, his sister felt that Mark would degrade himself by marrying into a Hasidic family."

"I understand, I understand. Those Assimilationists look down on us Orthodox. They believe that Jewish women wearing wigs and Jewish men with beards and sidecurls, wearing *beckishes* (dark garments like dressing gowns) trigger anti-Semitism. They speak only Polish and think they're big shots."

"Yes, they want to be known as true Poles—"

"And they call such a learned God-fearing Jew a *Chniok* (religious fanatic)."

"I can see that you know. Anyway, Mark has character. He disregarded his sister's warnings and her threats and before he was to leave Niemirov to take another job, he asked my parents for my hand."

"He must love you very much."

Her remark made me happy. "Can you imagine?" I said. "My parents refused him categorically. My father told him that as long as he lives he'll never permit me to marry him. To me he said that Mark was twice my age and could be my father. Everyone talks of his age as if he were fifty years old. He's only thirty-six, and I'm telling you, I wouldn't care any less if he were a hundred years old. I love him. The truth of the matter is that my parents didn't want a son-in-law who is assimilated and can't speak Yiddish."

She turned to me full-face and asked: "But, God forbid, he's not a Goy?"

"No. He's Jewish. Nevertheless, he and my father are worlds apart, because Mark wants to know nothing about Jewish life. My father, on the other hand, is like all Hasidim, very Orthodox."

She withdrew her hand from my shoulder and made herself comfortable on the wooden edge of the bed.

"Mark," I went on, "said that we certainly don't want to wait until my father dies, and suggested that we go to Lvov and get married there without the consent of our parents. For years I had resented being treated like a child. Here an opportunity presented itself to show my parents and sisters that I am a *person*, and able to make my own decisions. So, we eloped."

The woman shook her head in dismay and said, "Is that so, is that so."

"I asked Father for permission to visit Gina. She's a cousin of mine living in Lvov. That's how I got away from home. Unexpectedly, Mark's boss kept him two extra days in Niemirov which fouled up our plans. We got married just the same but we had no time for a honeymoon in Lvov. You do believe me?"

"I believe you, of course I believe you, child."

I wiped my eyes and concluded: "Before we separated for a whole year, we wanted to be together...don't you understand?"

"Why do you have to separate?"

"Mark made all the plans. We're supposed to keep our marriage a secret until he's prepared to take his final exams and be in a position to open his own law office. Meanwhile I'm returning to my parents."

A flicker of disapproval swept over her clean-scrubbed face, increasing my feelings of guilt and self-pity. "Perhaps I should have waited for Father to change his mind?" I burst into tears again and fell into the woman's arms.

"What about your mother, don't you have one?" the woman asked, wiping her own tears on her striped apron.

"I have a mother but she's always against me."

"No mother is against her child," she said.

My head left the comfort of her soft bosom, and looking directly into her face I said, "Mine is."

The door suddenly opened and in came the same policeman who had earlier taken Mark away.

"Where is my husband?" I asked.

"He's not your husband," he replied. "One of my colleagues took him to Linzer. You, girlie, dress and come to the station with me."

"I'm not going. I didn't do anything wrong. I'm going to wait for my husband right here!"

"He's not your husband and you know it. I must protect you from his dirty hands. You're going with me to the police station even if I have to handcuff you. Get dressed, hurry!"

"I swear that we are husband and wife."

"Then why did you arrive in town at night, ha? And for what purpose did you come to Komarov, ha? You came to a town where you have no relatives, no friends, why?"

In my mind I searched desperately for a plausible reason which could convince the policeman that there was nothing improper in Mark's relationship with me, that I needed no protection, but I could find nothing. Finally I burst out with the truth, hoping for his compassion.

"We were married against the will of my parents, that's why we haven't as yet got a civil marriage license. Please..."

He drowned out the rest of my words with a loud guffaw, almost choking on his own words: "All of them are alike. They all have stories to tell. What imaginations they have!"

"Please," I begged. "Telephone the police in Lvov. Get them to send an officer to Gina Fand. She is holding my Jewish marriage license. She will show it and we'll be cleared."

"Another woman," he laughed. "There's always another woman. Now, get dressed! Get going!"

"How can I get dressed with you here?" I said. And turning to the proprietress who was about to leave, I said: "Please stay."

"Don't play the innocent, ha? Get dressed and better make it snappy. Otherwise I'll drag you out just as you are."

I pulled off the nightgown under the cover of the feather-quilt and dressed under it at a snail's pace, hoping that at any moment Mark would return.

The policeman helped me into my coat, then shoved me out of the room and out of the hotel.

The snow was sharply white and crisp under my feet. The streets were deserted. He pulled me along to keep pace with his fast stride. I stumbled and, when he helped me to regain my balance, I hoped that time and the fresh air were beginning to have a sobering effect upon him.

He stopped in front of a small frame house with a small light burning over a sign, POLICJA. The house was otherwise dark. The policeman opened the door with his own key, pushed me in and switched on the light.

I remained near the door. My hope that he had sobered faded. He could hardly find his way to the desk. When he did, he slumped heavily into a chair and summoned me to come closer.

I started out slowly, then stopped as a mixture of odors, sweat, and alcohol assailed my nostrils. In his puffy face, his inflamed eyes had half closed. He blinked them open for a second and said: "Don't be afraid, little pigeon. You're under my protection now. The old wolf can't harm you now, ha? Poor girl. Why, you're almost a child."

"I am not a child. I am a married woman!"

"So, you don't want to be helped, ha?" He lunged forward and quickly pulled me onto his lap.

The suddenness of his movement startled me; the stench of his breath was sickening. I struggled to break away, but his grip was too strong. With one hand I kept his face away from mine, with the other I wrestled his hand fumbling at my skirt. "What's the matter, little pigeon, don't you like *young* men? Other girls do."

"Please let me go," I begged, feeling that my strength was ebbing.

It was clear to me that this chair had more than once been the means to a quick little affair.

I screamed.

"You go right ahead. It's more fun. Yell! Yell louder. It does something to me. Nobody can hear you. Nobody, I said. We're all alone. Nobody around. So, you don't like me, little pigeon, ha? You'll learn."

Steps clearly crunching in the snow came to my ears. "Somebody is coming!" I said.

He listened, and his hold loosened somewhat. I pushed hard against him. The chair was now off balance and when he reached out to the desk to save himself from falling along with the tumbling chair, I jerked free.

Somebody knocked at the door.

"Damn it! Another minute..." the policeman cursed out. But he quickly picked up the chair and collected himself. Another knock, and the policeman stood, hand on knob, impatiently waiting until I straightened my skirt and buttoned up my coat. He unlocked the door. Another policeman entered, followed by Mark and his colleague, Dr. Linzer. Linzer looked around suspiciously, eyeing me with more than a passing glance.

After considerable arguing, he somehow reached the policeman's befogged reasoning power, convincing him that Mark was not a seducer of a minor.

"How am I going to believe that they're married when they have no proof?"

"Let them go. I vouch for them. This should be more than enough for you."

"Maybe you're just eager to help them, ha? One lawyer is loyal to another," the policeman still argued, but only as if he wanted to save face.

"Let them go," Dr. Linzer said. "First thing in the morning you may institute an investigation. Should your findings prove my statement wrong, I myself will deliver them. All right?" He held out his hand to him.

The policeman slapped his open palm against Linzer's. Both laughed, shook hands like peasants in the Market Place after concluding an important deal.

# 4

*To obey out of love is better
than to obey out of fear.*

Rashi, *Commentaries on the Pentateuch,
Deuteronomy*

On the way back to the hotel Mark swore revenge.
"I'll file suit against the police of Komarov, against that drunkard, I'll see to it that he loses his job." He continued his tirade until I reminded him that under the circumstances this would not be the rational thing to do.

"Our secret will be out, and what will my parents do to me?"

"I don't give a damn so long as that imbecile gets what's coming to him."

It surprised me that Mark didn't ask how I happened to be in the police station. Did my face reveal nothing of the dreadful struggle I had gone through a short time ago, nothing of the revulsion I had felt?

Linzer had noticed. He had even looked closely at the policeman and had asked if I was all right.

But as we walked on, I reasoned that Mark was too angry to be observant, and perhaps justifiably so. His pride was hurt; he remembered only his own humiliation. I snuggled closer to him and said: "My dear, let's forget it all for now. We have so little time left, so very little."

Tearing himself away from me, he cried out: "No! I won't forget. Those insults! Never in my life have I been so humiliated. You wait and see!"

The proprietress was sitting in the bar warming her hands over a firepot, as if waiting for us. I felt a great need for a bath and asked if she could prepare one. It was almost midnight, she said. She would have to bring up coal from the cellar, make a fire, heat the water on the stove and carry it to the tub. She promised to have a bath ready for me first thing in the morning.

The room we came back to almost seemed cozy now. I threw off my clothes and slipped into bed where Mark was already waiting for me. He embraced me and I snuggled closer and I felt secure. But, when he started to make love to me, the incident with the policeman struck me with full force in all its ugly details. Nor did Mark's jabbering about his plans for revenge have any more appeal for me now than it had earlier. His embrace felt too tight; his head pressed against my shoulder felt too heavy...

I slept little and dreaded the thought of returning to Niemirov where I would have to face my parents. In the morning I gathered enough courage to ask Mark to take me along to Cracow.

"How can I? I have only a furnished room there."

"That's enough for me."

"What will people say, a man of my standing, living with his wife in a furnished room?"

"Isn't being together more important than gossip?"

"No, it isn't. We'll have to wait until I open my own law office."

"But—"

"Stop it," he said. "I know what I'm doing. I don't want to hear any more of your nonsense." Then in a much softer tone of voice: "Darling, we talked about it so many times, leave it to me. It won't be as bad as it seems right now. As soon as I'm settled in my new job, I'll start looking for another, closer to Niemirov, so that we'll be able to see each other from time to time. And just as soon as the year is over, I'll ask your father's blessing again, and should he refuse again, I'll simply tell him we're already married. Regardless of his answer, we'll be together from then on. Let me see you smile, Darling." He clenched his fist, pushed up my chin and asked: "Will you be patient until then? Will you write every day?"

He was older, he was wiser, he knew better. "I will, I will," I said.

The proprietress called to us that the driver was waiting to take Mark to the station.

I embraced him so passionately that his glasses dropped, but I was able to catch them before they fell to the floor. When I apologized, his stern face flashed a forgiving smile. He kissed me and rushed out of the room.

I caught up with him in the bar and embraced him once more, in full view of the early morning customers.

# 5

*The present is never an object
of purpose; the past and present
are our mediums to attain the purpose.*

*Blaise Pascal*

In the train, on my way from Komarov to Lvov, sandwiched between two men, I listened to the monotonous rhythm of the turning wheels. Exhausted and sleepy, my eyelids drooped over my eyes, but somehow I couldn't fall asleep. The prospect of having to face my parents and live with them for a whole year, constantly pretending, hovered threateningly over me. Pretending was putting it mildly. I had gone to Lvov supposedly to visit Gina and now I would have to concoct more lies; a terrible violation of my father's teachings.

Father had gained his wisdom from talmudic books which he studied every minute away from the business. He derived deep pleasure from it as well as knowledge which had earned him the respect of Jew and Gentile alike. Or had he won the respect of the people because he set for himself and his family so high a standard of ethics? But this, too, was clearly the result of being passionately devoted to the teachings in the holy volumes. There was a permanent tie between him and the books, as though they were his lifeline.

He tried to imbue his children with the same passion for the holy books and what they conveyed. Each time one of us, by coincidence, dropped a Hebrew book we had to pick it up and kiss the cover as if apologizing for our carelessness.

I wondered: How would it be possible for me to conceal my marriage from this straightforward man? I prayed that he would be away upon my return, on the job, supervising his laborers in building a road to Rava-Ruska.

Father had inherited the business of the repair and construction of highways from his father. By the time he had taken it over, the business was flourishing. Roads in Poland were poor in general and around Niemirov they were always in need of repair. One of Father's other projects was to buy forests, cut down the trees to sell part for building and part for fuel. He had the reputation of being exceptionally lucky in his business dealings.

My mother had opened a textile store against my father's advice. He wanted her to be a homemaker only. Her store was successful. She divided her time between the business and her son Alexander, stricken with rickets.

The whole family, three sisters and another brother, knew that the boxes of oranges imported from Italy were meant for Alexander only. No one resented the love Mother lavished upon the sick boy. Not even I who longed desperately for some token of her affection. But she never kissed me. She never embraced me. Her hand never stroked my hair.

Often I would envy my friend Ethel when I witnessed the tenderness with which her mother caressed her. I suppose that she sensed something of my feelings because sometimes she would go out of her way to be affectionate toward me, even if it were only to pat my shoulder or pinch my cheek. When she would do this, automatically the day would brighten. I accepted her friendship with gratitude, yet it deepened my sadness for what was lacking at home.

Alexander died when he was fourteen. All of us felt his loss. Mother's grief was beyond words. She wept whenever his name was mentioned. She wept at other times also. Eventually she transferred the care she had given Alexander to his twin-sister Blume, a girl of delicate health who was five years my junior.

Father retreated into his spiritual world, further engrossing himself in the study of the Talmud. Every day he was wakened at five o'clock in the morning by the sexton who knocked at our door, as he did at the door of each Jewish house surrounding the Market Place. Father quickly dressed and rushed to the *shul*. There, together with others, or by himself, he studied. By nine o'clock he was back for breakfast, never forgetting first to pour milk into the fat cat's dish. Tin-Tin followed him like a dog. She would rub her white fur against Father's shoes. When, on rare occasions, he picked her up she meowed happily.

He seemed his old self again. Didn't he miss his son? The only clue to his feelings was his remark to Mother: "You shouldn't cry so much. God has a purpose in everything. It was His will." Did his Hasidic sect teach him only to see the shining light and to close his eyes as soon as shadows obsured the sun? He even transformed his everyday bodily functions to serve as hymns to God, and thus derived tranquility.

I always knew for a fact that my father loved me but he embraced me for the first time when I was about thirteen. I had looked forward to beginning the onset of menstruation, believing that this would make me a member of the adult world and automatically improve the relationship between my two older sisters and myself. I had never had any important problems with my younger sister Blume nor with my older brother Abner. And Mother, too, would no longer treat me as a child. I had made a resolve to tell her of my loneliness during an intimate talk we would have in the isolation of the special room behind the master bedroom where all serious conversations took place. I had hoped she would change her hostile attitude.

I was deeply disappointed when the important day finally arrived. Mother evaded my questions by referring me to my oldest sister. "Go to Anna," she said. "Anna will take care of you. I haven't the time. A customer is waiting in the store."

Anna explained the menstrual cycle in a few words and returned to her book, *Burning Paris*, by the popular author Bruno Jasienski.

That evening I fainted.

Father took me in his arms, carried me into my parents' bedroom and didn't relax his hold until I was safely on top of his high bed, all the while murmuring: "What's the matter, my child? What's the matter, Roma?" Then he raised his voice, "Anna, water! Bring water quickly!"

Anna brought water. He dipped his hand and brushed my face gently. His strong embrace, his cool moist hand resting on my forehead, his soft voice full of concern calling my name, gave me a sense of security I had never known before. I heard and saw all this through a haze, wishing the moments would expand into hours. I felt relieved.

Several hours later I fainted again. Once more Father carried me into the bedroom. His baritone voice conveyed a message of deep affection for me. "What's the matter, Roma?"

Before he had a chance to tell Anna or Adela to fetch a doctor, Mother entered the bedroom. "Lejzor," she said, "you don't have to fuss over her, she's faking."

"Perhaps she is. But if one is faking sickness, one is indeed sick."

Each time I fainted Father consoled me with his strong hold and gentle touch and concerned voice, urging one of my sisters to call a doctor. Later he would again enter the room on tiptoe, bending over me so close that his red beard almost touched my face, His deep-blue eyes looking sadly at me, he would ask: "How do you feel, my child, better?"

I was deeply moved and promised myself never again to yield to my weakness. However, when loneliness choked me, I would faint.

Despite my father's obvious love, he often rebuked me. Each time I went out with a boy, it was embarrassing to him. Girls were not supposed to meet boys unless their parents arranged such meetings with a serious purpose in mind.

"We've plenty of time for that," he would say. "You're only a child. You have two older sisters and you have an older brother. Only after they are married can we think of boys for you."

He also scolded me for riding my bicycle on Saturday before the appearance of three stars in the sky indicating that the Sabbath was over. Father compressed a great deal of meaning into a few words, and his politely expressed wish carried more weight than a rigid order ever could.

It made me sad to see his handsome face drawn, his large eyes under his thick, black eyebrows looking wistfully at me, motioning me into the isolated room. He took a snuffbox from his coat pocket, sniffed, sneezed, but not as heartily as usual. Then he dabbed his nose with a plaid handkerchief, and finally asked me whether it was true that I had eaten ham with a group of teenagers in the little forest on Rava-Ruska Street.

Hurt by his distress, I lied: "It's not true, I swear! You can ask Ethel Galler (grandchild of a rabbi), she'll tell you that I didn't."

"I don't want any witnesses, I believe you rather than what people tell me in the *shul*."

I bent my head.

He was against letting me go to Lvov where I wanted to enroll in high school. Girls, in his opinion, didn't need much of an education. This privilege was reserved for boys. My argument that Anna had graduated from high school and that Adela had finished Handelsakademie (advanced business school) did not change his mind. "They," he said, "took advantage of the schools that were in Vienna, where we lived at that time."

Anna's husband, Hersh, whom she had properly met through a matchmaker, helped me influence Father. Hersh, himself a Hasid like Father, to my surprise was very knowledgeable without ever having attended secular schools. Later he was also to help bridge the differences between my father and myself which enabled me to go to Lvov.

In Lvov I had shared a room with Gina, a cousin and dear friend. Her stepmother, Klara, a young, beautiful widow, was her guardian and she became mine too. She seldom reprimanded us for coming home after ten, did not press us to do our homework, and allowed us to choose our friends without interference.

Although the straitjacket had loosened in these new surroundings, it was still a man's world, and I promised myself that one day I would shed my shackles. Hoping to gain a comrade-in-arms, I refused to let Gina ignore or brush aside even the smallest difference in treatment or attitude we girls would receive.

Gina was gay and witty, and seemed to me to be very sophisticated—perhaps because she had two beaus. Artur, who had little education, showed his love for her with gifts, which she accepted graciously. The other, Paul, studying architecture at the Politechnica, stimulated her intellectually, she claimed.

Both firmly believed in her affection, neither knowing about the other. Even when Artur got an inkling of Paul's role in Gina's life, her wit saved her from a showdown and both remained her ardent admirers. Many times she asked me to keep Artur, the generous one, company until she returned from a date with Paul, the student.

Many books about sex were available to the girls in my circle. I had read *Sexual Questions* by August Forel and *Ideal Marriage* by Van de Velde, and had discussed them with the other girls. I was convinced that I knew a great deal about sex, but somehow when Gina and I spoke about it, it became different. Her big, green eyes focused on me changed color. They became brownish, as her voice deepened. Her transformation excited me. I felt almost as if I were participating in her love adventures.

After graduation I felt like a stranger in Niemirov, a town with only three thousand inhabitants. I missed Gina, school, and the freedom I had enjoyed in Lvov. Niemirov was almost isolated from the rest of Poland, since the only means of transportation to the nearest large city, Lvov, was a bus running once a day. Life was injected into the community by the people who came from other parts of the country to treat their rheumatism in the sulphur and mud baths for which Niemirov had its reputation.

During the season, which lasted three months, movies were shown, horse races took place, and a band of five musicians played twice daily in the resort park. After the season closed, the town went to sleep.

I longed to travel to distant places like Vienna, my birthplace, and especially to America. *Lincoln's Biography* by Emil Ludwig had stirred my curiosity. However, there was little prospect of my ever getting there because it was so far from my homeland. Nonetheless I fed my aroused interest with books by Jack London and Sinclair Lewis, and dreamed up strange events which would diminish my despair over Father's reprimands, and I wrote what I then believed was poetry.

I decided to run away.

Knowing that money would be a necessity in my plans, I now deprived myself of visits to the local candy store. Mother had occasionally given me money for books or candy.

I saved the fifty groszen or frequently a zloty that I avoided spending. On certain occasions I had the opportunity to steal a zloty or two. Money was not tight at home. When enough coins accumulated, I'd exchange them in the post office for a five-zloty bill, sneak up to the attic, lift a wooden floor board which was loosely attached to the beam and stashed the bill there. This vault, between the ceiling of my parents' bedroom and the floor of the attic, became an expedient device for replenishing my hope for a better future. It made it easier for me to bear the restrictions and to endure the boredom of small town life.

I felt comfortable being left at home alone. This made it possible for me to write without being ridiculed. I could go to the attic without the fear of being discovered. There I indulged in the pleasure of counting and recounting my treasure, trying to estimate the date when I would have accumulated eighty zlotys, the monthly earnings of a white-collar employee. That amount, I believed, would carry me through the period of job hunting in my new city. Once employed, I would save and skimp until I had enough for college. I wanted to study journalism more than anything in the world. Then, like a man, I would be freer to move about, make a living for myself, and control my own destiny. I would no longer feel like a prisoner whose life could be decided upon at the whim of her family or some other force beyond her control.

For most Jews in Poland it was not yet considered acceptable for unmarried girls of a *Yichus* family (scholarly heritage) to work outside the home unless it was in a family business. Therefore these plans had to be kept from anyone's knowledge.

Although I had inspected my "vault" in the attic only two days before, I went there again. I counted the bills, finding it hard to believe that I had already amassed sixty zlotys, and that my date of departure was growing closer. Next fall I might be ready. Liberation was in sight.

I replaced the wooden board and crept down the stairs leading to the corridor which had an exit to the street. Exhilarated, I forgot that secrecy was superfluous, since no one was home. Absorbed in my thoughts, I stole out through the back way, and bumped into a stranger. Only then did I realize my odd behavior and answered to his *"Przepraszam bardzo"* (excuse me) with "It was my fault."

My inquiries concerning the stranger in town revealed his name, his profession, his age, and his whereabouts. Our formal introduction took place the following evening in the candy store.

He was Mark Rathauser, now my husband.

# 6

*Don't worry about tomorrow;
who knows what will befall you today?*

Talmud: Yebamoth, 63b

Slowly, the train pulled into the Lvov Station. The anticipation of seeing Gina Fand was comforting. Didn't she know the answer to all problems?

Gina embraced me in the foyer. She stepped back to look at me and said: "You seem to be wrapped in a cloud. What's the matter, Roma?"

In her room, the same one I had shared during high school years, she asked me innumerable questions—all revolving around the honeymoon. "Remember our vow, Roma, to tell each other *everything*?"

I told her, but mostly emphasizing the incident with the policeman. "I am afraid to go home. Maybe that policeman has already informed the police in Niemirov. Maybe my parents already know that I'm married."

"So what?" Gina laughed, and her face took on a mischievous expression. "If I were you I'd tell them myself."

"Never! I promised Mark to keep it a secret. I could never betray his trust."

"Have it your way, but don't worry so much. Everything will straighten out—you'll see."

# 7

*Love lives on small amiabilities.*

Theodor Fontane

Back home, I ran to the post office every day to pick up the letters Mark would mail to me. Though burdened by the secret, it also gave me an air of importance.

However, both lasted only a short time.

Four weeks had elapsed when my father came home from evening prayer looking reproachfully at me. He motioned for me to follow him to the rear of the house into the isolated room. Nervously curling one black sidelock, he asked me in a trembling voice whether it was true that I had married Mark Rathauser.

I rememberd very well my promise to Mark, yet I could not withstand the searching eyes of my father.

"Yes, it is true," I whispered, and wished he could not hear me.

His face turned ashen in the yellow light of the kerosene lamp. He slumped into a chair muttering in a soft voice: "Why should God punish me so? I should have known all along that nothing good would come of you. One among four daughters, one among all girls in town, preaching equality with men... To embarrass your sister Adela and your brother Abner who are older than you! To marry before them, and on top of it, an atheist."

"He's not an atheist."

"And what is he? Does he possibly go to *shul*? Reb Alter told me he doesn't. Not even on Atonement Day. Does he perhaps speak Yiddish? He doesn't. Might he be able to read the holy books? No. What kind of a Jew is he anyway?"

"He doesn't go to *shul*," I admitted, "He can't read Hebrew and can't speak Yiddish—but he is a Jew."

Father, wringing his hands, left the room without another word.

I blew the light out and remained sitting in the dark. It was true that both Adela and Abner, older than myself, might be embarrassed. It was customary for children to marry in consecutive order. When a younger sister married first, ugly superstition claimed that the older would never marry. I knew that Abner was in love with Sara Frankel the poorest girl in town, and after the wedding would move into our home with Sara and become a business partner with father. But what about Adela? Educated Adela, speaking several languages fluently, yet having difficulty developing friendships with even the *girls* in Niemirov. Did I do harm to her? Would she ever forgive me? But how could I have known that the secret I wanted to keep for a whole year would come out so soon?

It must have been *Reb* Alter who told Father. *Reb* Alter had appointed himself watchman over the morals of every Jew in town. One had to measure up to the standards of his Hasidic sect. Many a parent's repudiation of his teenaged offspring was inspired by *Reb* Alter. Often some of them refrained from greater leniency only because of his watchful eye. By some uncanny means, he was always the first to spot the trespasser. Elders respected him for his knowledge and his strict adherence to the Hasidic law; most of the young despised him.

Of course it was *Reb* Alter who had informed and inflamed my father! Then I had to admit to myself that I had made *Reb* Alter the scapegoat. I knew very well that Father had a mind of his own, and was as ardent a Hasid as *Reb* Alter; the only difference between their actions was that Father never interfered in other people's problems unless he was asked for advice.

My heart ached seeing Father suffer. I told myself that this was the price I had to pay while struggling for progress. But this reasoning did not reduce the self-flagellation. I was selfish in pursuing my own goals, my own happiness. I dismissed the fleeting thought that no compromise short of divorce would be too great a sacrifice if only I could banish Father's unhappiness.

Mother and Father came in, both engaged in a heated discussion. "Shall we put her out, bag and baggage?" I heard Mother say. Then a match scratched against a matchbox, a flickering light lit the kerosene lamp.

I rose to leave, embarrassed to have heard a fragment of a confidential conversation between my parents.

Mother noticed me first, gave me a passing glance, adjusted her brown wig, and went right back through the door. Her thin lips under her fleshy upturned nose opened slightly, in a smile or grimace, showing a few of her gold-covered teeth. Father followed her out. I wondered more than ever what charms she might have had in her youth that had made Father want her. Still, I wished more than ever that she would return, smiling warmly, or that she would say a kind word, perhaps touch me with her rough hands. But the only part of her that remained in the room was the strong scent of laundry soap.

# 8

*Someone drowning will reach
even for a razorblade.*

*Hasidic saying*

Twice a year my father went to a Tzaddik (Righteous One), also referred to as *Rebbe*, residing in Belz, one of the oldest towns in Poland.

The *Rebbe*'s Hasidim believed beyond any doubt that his supernatural powers came directly from God, and so they swarmed into Belz from all over the country: from Hungary, Rumania, and other countries they would come for an audience that might last for only a few minutes. They asked for advice in business matters, whether or not a forthcoming marriage met with his approval, and which doctor to choose for an operation. They asked for the *Rebbe*'s blessing, and yearned to listen to a few words of his wisdom.

He was one among the few exceptionally great minds able to indulge in the study of the Cabala. Those informed claimed that minds short of genius are incapable of absorbing the depth of this secret study and as a result of it crack up.

The suggestions of the *Rebbe* were strictly followed and his Hasidim returned home spiritually revived, with new strength to face their many problems, poverty being the root of most of them.

They felt at peace after the *Rebbe* showed them a way, as if indeed he had taken the burden of decision-making and responsibility off their heavy hearts. Although the *Rebbe* himself needed little, for he fasted more days than he ate, the voluntary lifetime commitment to contribute to his upkeep never failed.

Father also journeyed to see the *Rebbe* as often as an emergency situation arose. Such a situation had arisen and had nothing to do with me.

A government investigation was pending against my father as to the quality of the stone and workmanship he had used on the road to Rava-Ruska.

Two engineers had come from the main Road Building Office located in Lvov to check the roadside. They stopped in our house to inform Father about the intended inspection.

Unfortunately it was Saturday and my father told them that he never did business on the Sabbath.

The engineers were astonished because they had provided Father with an opportunity to be there and to explain or perhaps prove the accusation to be unfounded.

The engineers left.

Outside, walking towards their waiting car, I overheard them say: "...is a fool, doesn't he realize what's at stake? Yet somehow I respect that damn Jew..." They drove away.

Father was troubled and began to make preparations for a trip to Belz.

Try as I would, until now, I could not make my parents understand or accept my marriage to the assimilated lawyer husband of mine. Perhaps the *Rebbe* could help? We could tell him of my "crime" and let him be the judge.

It was I who asked Father to take me along for a *Din-Torah* (judgement by the law of the Torah). I promised that I would abide by the *Rebbe*'s decision no matter what it might be.

Father was perplexed. Roma, his daughter who always rebelled against religious rites and practices and hid from rituals, was willing to let the *Rebbe* decide her future fate? Now she would trust the ultimate authority of everything she defied? Father was confused. Not knowing that I was doing it only for his love and for restoring his peace of mind, he could do nothing but agree.

# 9

*Sages are more important than kings,
for if a sage dies, who can replace him?
When a king dies all Israel
is eligible to succeed him.*

*Adapted from the Midrash*

The wooden sidewalks of Belz were crowded with so many Hasidim that it was difficult to push through. There were no rooms, not even beds to be had anywhere. As a last resort we went to distant relatives and they were willing to share beds with us.

The *Rebbe* lived in a spacious but modest house, with an interior bare of all decoration. Yet, I felt that I had entered into a princely mansion. Close to the *Rebbe*'s chamber, his Hasidic staff behaved in a hushed, regal manner.

Not so in the waiting room. It was filled with Jews—men, women and children—who were in need of being consoled, advised, unburdened, healed, and blessed. Some were praying, some weeping, some groaning, some talking. Some were sitting as though in a stupor. Many came back day after day hoping to be called into the *Rebbe*'s chamber, longing to be alone with him for a little while at least.

Off the long corridor were a few rooms that housed the *Rebbe*'s family and live-in attendants. It was considered a great honor to serve the *Rebbe*. Many volunteered their services free of charge and had to fight for the privilege. They believed in pursuing a heavenly cause by protecting the *Rebbe* from any involvement in trivial matters so that he might dwell in his world of spirit and holiness. It was his divine calling to be occupied with big or small troubles of people who needed him.

My oldest sister's father-in-law, Shaje Halbertal—nicknamed Shaje Raver after his hometown—was one of the honorary attendants. He spent most of his time at the side of the Belzer *Rebbe* as a sort of secretary. Father asked for him, but was told that Shaje was at an important conference with a Polish political delegation. After a while, he emerged with three distinguished looking Poles heading for the exit. He bowed a few times and shook hands with them at parting.

It was common knowledge that some Polish political factions sent their delegations to bargain for votes before election; to make deals with the *Rebbe*. But they never passed the threshold of *his* chamber. He was never to be bothered by secular matters. It was his representative, Shaje Raver, or someone like him, who promised to influence the Hasidim to vote for some particular political candidate. He was promised, in return, to get a law passed which was important to the ways of life for the Orthodox Jew. The Polish delegation enhanced the deal by also granting a few licenses for liquor and tobacco stores if they won the election. These, the *Rebbe* distributed among the poorest, dipping into his own treasury to pay for the initial merchandise. There was a saying: "Belz takes from the rich and gives to the poor."

Shaje Raver, owner of a lucrative textile business in Rava-Ruska run by his family, went home at irregular intervals. His wife and his two sons had the pleasure of his company only when he needed money for contributions or for his personal expenses. The Halbertal family not only approved Shaje's honorary job but were very proud of it. He was a most devout disciple, ready to give his life for the revered and beloved *Tzaddik*.

Five years later, when the Germans occupied all of Poland, the *Rebbe*'s faithful brought him from Belz to Przemyslany. Upon learning of his presence, local Ukrainians informed the Nazis of his whereabouts. They rushed to the hiding place and encountering a distinguished looking Hasid, they mistakenly took for the *Rebbe*. They beat him up mercilessly, and threw him down a flight of stairs. After Josie Singer, the victim of mistaken identity, had regained consciousness, he said: "I am happy that God chose me to suffer instead of the *Rebbe*."

Then the Nazis went on a rampage, rounded up about forty Jews, including Moshe Rokeach, the son of the *Rebbe*, locked them up in the local synagogue and set the building on fire.

Years after the war, his close disciples wondered why the *Rebbe*, knowing the exact date of his son's death, never observed his *Jahrzeit* (death anniversary). They dared not ask questions, but they presumed that he did not want to make use of a privilege which his fellow survivors did not have.

The *Rebbe* was brought from Przemyslany first to one and then to another hiding place. Finally, the necessary contacts were made, an astronomical amount of money was paid, and the *Rebbe* was masqueraded as a badly wounded officer of high rank. Even his face was bandaged. He was smuggled to the Hungarian border, was met by Hungarian-Jewish authorities and escorted safely across the frontier. It was rumored that the *Rebbe* escaped from Hungary to Palestine with the active help of Admiral Horthy, the Regent himself.

While still on the run from the Germans, on his stay in the Cracow ghetto, the *Rebbe* was besieged by his people whose trust in his clairvoyance and wisdom was strong and unshaken. One of them was Arik Weintraub. His only wish was that his three-year-old son should survive. A rare opportunity came his way. Izio Green, his brother-in-law, found a Polish Catholic who was willing to take in little Bernie. All arrangments were made to smuggle the child out of the ghetto. But, before the painful separation was to take place, Arik Weintraub went to the Belzer *Rebbe*, told him of the plan and asked for his blessing. The *Rebbe* blessed them and stated that "not a hair of Bernie's head will be harmed." Believing it was an assurance that his son would survive any circumstances he decided not to accept the chance offered by Izio Green. The family remained together and survived. Arik believes that the Belzer *Rebbe* and his blessing paved the way to their survival.

In the Belzer *Rebbe's* anteroom, I heard groans of pain coming from one corner, wailing from another. The chatter of some people mingled with the constant whining of an infant. Attendants and paid staff, all in long, black kaftans with beards and sidelocks, appeared and disappeared through various doors leading to the inner rooms. Only one door was watched closely. When it opened from the inside at about half-hour intervals, the chattering and groaning stopped and the mother hushed the whining baby. In the silence, all signs of life were suspended, everybody looked at the *gabbe* Aaron Shije, framed in the doorway and calling out a name. The person would rush nervously toward him. After the door shut behind them, the noise exploded again as though a dam had burst with the onslaught of water.

A boy of about twelve, on crutches, led by his well-dressed, attractive mother, came in. She seated the boy on the bench next to me. Covering his knees with a plaid blanket, she asked me: "Where do you come from?"

"Niemirov."

"Niemirov? I know Niemirov, it's the resort place," she said. And after a while: "Have you been waiting a long time? We arrived in Belz three days ago. We're from Rzeszov. Do you know Rzeszov?" Without waiting for an answer, she went on: "Every morning we come here to await our turn. I was definitely promised an audience today. We're lucky at that, aren't we, Mendele? Other people have to wait much longer."

The boy nodded, but kept staring out the window while rolling his blond curly sidelocks.

Pulling the blanket up to his hips, his mother continued: "It's no wonder that the Belzer *Rebbe* has so many followers. Take myself. Two years ago I was sick, I thought I would die. I came to Belz and you can see the miracle for yourself. Do I look like a sick person? I'm well and if I take it easy, the doctor said, I can live to a-hundred-twenty."

"What was your sickness?"

"What do you mean what was my sickness? I had heart failure, of course. The *Rebbe* gave me his blessing and referred me to a specialist in Lvov. Though I live in Rzeszov—and believe you me, we have plenty of fine doctors in Rzeszov—I went to Dr. Tanne in Lvov and he cured me just like the *Rebbe* said he would. But now, look, it must be the evil eye, look at my sorrow. My boy, my only child is sick." Tears that came suddenly to her eyes just as suddenly disappeared. "But I know," she said with a sigh, "and so does Mendele, that with the *Rebbe*'s blessing he'll get well, he'll get well."

While she was chattering I could not tear my gaze away from a very poorly dressed woman sitting near the window rocking the whining baby. Despair in her face, her tearful eyes focused on that special mahogany door, she jumped to her feet each time it opened. She had been assured of priority on account of her infant. When Aaron Shije apologized to her from the distance, gesturing with his arms spreading apart and calling someone else for an audience, she slumped in her chair, never ceasing to rock the baby.

Finally he called her. She disappeared into the room leading to the *Rebbe*'s chambers. Twenty-five minutes later she returned.

The change in her appearance was incredible. She was no longer crying and the baby was no longer whining. Her luminous face, her walk conveyed a self-confidence as though she was in a hurry to get to her heavenly destination. Even her gray coat, too thin to keep her warm, no longer seemed shabby.

I didn't believe in miracles or in supernatural powers. To me, the *Rebbe* was the product of many generations of his kind. Each transmitted to the succeeding member a knowledge of the Torah and a peculiarly specialized wisdom adapted to handling Jewish problems. His parents and his grandparents before him had had more experience in dealing with people than most psychiatrists, because they had witnessed so much daily misery. I attributed the *Rebbe*'s profound insight into human nature to his extraordinary sensitivity, perception and deep compassion. The *Rebbe* was the rich, as well as the poor, man's psychiatrist, a friend and advisor to both; and most important, he had some inner power which triggered in his disciples an extraordinary love for the teachings of the Torah.

Father, being an ardent follower and a generous contributor to the maintenance of the *Rebbe*'s office, enjoyed his special friendship. Once when the *Rebbe* came to Niemirov he stayed in Moshe Schall's spacious villa but he chose to eat in our house, the greatest honor a Hasid could dream of. This factor and Shaje Raver's influence spared us from waiting for an audience for a few days. Father nudged me to be prepared; he expected to be summoned any minute.

Aaron Shije led us into the adjoining room, and the noise now filtered through as if it were an ocean gently lapping against the shore. The half-drawn window shades allowed ample light for Aaron Shije to make notes in handwriting. Both men conversed in soft voices, one urging to make it brief and the other pleading to have his problem elaborated more extensively on the *Quitle* (application).

Aaron Shije's glances in my direction made me aware that now my problem was on the agenda. I had no knowledge of this preliminary step before being admitted to the *Rebbe* himself. What if a decision depended on Aaron Shije's interpretation instead of the *Rebbe*'s own approach which I believed would be truly unbiased? What if Father was now influencing Aaron Shije, who in turn would present my case in such a way that the new verdict might compel me to divorce Mark?

Aaron Shije disappeared into an adjacent room. I did not speak to my father and I did not look at him. I could not have spoken anyway. My throat was locked, my head swimming. Here, my fate was to be decided. I should never have suggested this arbitration. Too much was at stake. Now it was too late to retreat. Aaron Shije reappeared, and led us to the sanctuary.

Bookcases filled with leather-bound volumes covered two walls. The Belzer *Rebbe* was sitting at the head of a long table, in the center of the room. His armchair was much too large for his small shrunken body. His head bent down, his chin resting against his chest, he looked like a thirteen-year-old boy. His transparent bluish eyelids opened only for brief moments. He rarely lifted his head, and when he did, his deep-set eyes were fixed at a point above my head.

Did he see me? Did he see my father? Perhaps he only partially perceived our presence. The main part of him remained in another region.

Aaron Shije placed the *Quitle*, which contained the outline of our problems on the table in front of the *Rebbe*. While reading, the *Rebbe* paused a few times during which he meditated, and after he finished reading he paused again. At just the moment I thought he had fallen asleep he addressed Father in a weak voice: "You are worried about your livelihood?"

Father nodded.

"Tell me, do you know who informed on you?"

"I know. A *Goy* who would like to take over my district."

The *Rebbe* shook his head and then asked in a louder tone of voice: "Why don't you offer the *Goy* a partnership?"

"A partnership? He knows nothing about road construction and, besides, I would have to share my profits with him."

"Half the profit is better than nothing," the *Rebbe* said. With a gesture he stopped Father from further arguments. "With the Almighty's help, everything will work out to your satisfaction."

A deep silence followed. I could hear the ticking of my wristwatch. The ascetic man hunched in the chair had again removed himself from us, from the room to which thousands of people would come after us to seek release from their emotional burdens. They relied on the *Rebbe*, who appeared so fragile. It was surprising that he could hold himself upright.

This man, at the other end of the table, had climbed to the spiritual summit, and would have preferred to remain there in seclusion were it not for all those people who needed his wisdom in their very earthly matters. Everyone is capable of experiencing a moment of spiritual elation, but he, Rokeach, could maintain himself in such a state of grace for most of the time had it not been for his attendants who seated him, in this room, in this overly large armchair, to serve; at this moment he served my father and me.

Once more his weak voice hardly carried to where I stood as he spoke of the second problem: "Does your daughter live with Mark, the son of Herman, in concubinage?"

"No. That's just it. She married him against my will."

"Did your daughter renounce her religion?"

"No. But this Mark is completely assimilated. He can't even speak Yiddish."

"Blessed be the Almighty," the *Rebbe* interrupted. "Go home in peace. Give your child the dowry you intended to give her had she married a man of your own choosing."

The audience was over. No protestations were thinkable, nor did anybody ever question the wisdom of the *Rebbe*'s conclusions. Whenever his advice produced favorable results for the petitioner, the sage was made responsible and received gratitude. For unfavorable results, the petitioner would blame himself for living a sinful life and not deserving any better. He would submit himself to more arduous repentance.

Aaron Shije appeared, to usher us out.

I turned my head before leaving the chamber to view once

more the man in the oversized armchair. What rare perseverance he needed to overcome the weariness and exhaustion of his frail physique. I felt deep compassion for him, this man who was so remote from my own stream of life.

Outside, Father wondered aloud about every word the *Rebbe* had uttered. Shaking his head in amazement, he said: "Can you imagine? The *Rebbe* knew even before I told him that someone babbled to the authorities. How could he know that Rostocki undermined me to get my business?" Absorbed in his thoughts, he had forgotten the direction to our quarters.

"This way, Father."

"Oh, yes. But why did he ask me to make him a partner? He knows everything, so he must know that Rostocki is a do-nothing. Still, he insisted."

The *Rebbe* may or may not know that Rostocki is a do-nothing, but he knows that he's a Pole and therefore could benefit your business, I thought, but didn't say it.

"Did you see how long the *Rebbe* looked at me when he gave me his blessing? Much longer than the last time, I can assure you. And I heard him with my own ears say that everything will work out to my satisfaction. It sounded like a real promise."

Father took no notice of my presence as we walked through snow and mud over the wooden sidewalks. He recalled every word and dwelled on it. He probed changes in the *Rebbe*'s intonation. He recalled every gesture and weighed each of them in different ways as to the importance of the meaning.

# 10

*Who's vindictive will be sorry,
who forgives will reap joy.*

*Hasidic saying*

Father obeyed the *Rebbe*'s verdict to the letter. Once home, he invited Mark, who meanwhile had taken a job in Rava-Ruska, twenty kilometers from Niemirov, to call. Mark entered our house reluctantly. Though I tried to be an intermediary and talk for both of them, it did not bring them much closer together.

"What are your plans?" Father asked him.

"Roma knows," Mark snapped.

"As soon as he opens his law office I will join him," I said.

"When will this be?"

"In a year's time."

Father's forehead wrinkled. "You heard what the *Rebbe* said. Man and wife should live together. How much do you need to set up a home, ten thousand or fifteen thousand zlotys?"

"In my position it would rather cost thirty thousand zlotys."

"Less wouldn't do?"

Blushing from embarrassment, I left the room. I was furious that Father had been so blunt; I was furious that Mark had discussed money matters in my presence.

I called Father out of the room.

He was unperturbed. "How will the cat cross the water? You want to be with your husband, don't you? So, things have to be arranged. Why should he feel insulted when he's offered money which will enable him to live a normal life together with his wife?"

Though the rest of the conversation between my father and Mark remained strained, interrupted by many silences, I hoped for improvement of their relationship in the future.

The three-thousand-dollar dowry Father gave us made it possible for Mark to give up his job and devote full time to study in preparation for the last exams after which he could open his own law ofice.

Father also contacted Mr. Rostocki and offered him fifty shares of his business. The Pole accepted the offer, an agreement was signed and the investigation was dropped. The Road Construction Office knew very well who really did the work, but all was well as long as Rostocki's name headed the reports. And Father regained every bit of the payments he gave to Rostocki by bidding higher and getting more contracts than ever before.

# 11

*Time produces and
time heals wounds.*

*Hasidic saying*

Three years later, after welcoming me and my two-year-old child, Mother asked me politely to sit down, a habit she had formed lately whenever I visited her. Evenings I often found her alone and perhaps she was lonely.

Adela—despite superstition—had married a local boy and was comfortably settled with her in-laws, as were Abner, his wife Sara and their one-year old Lisa, with our parents in an apartment upstairs. Every evening Father studied the Talmud in the synagogue and Blume, the unmarried youngest child, was out with her girl friends.

I pulled a chair close to the yellow light coming from a large kerosene lamp hanging on the wall above my mother's head. I thumbed through the *Chwila*, a Jewish newspaper published in the Polish language by a friend of mine, Henry Hescheles. At the same time I watched Bruno wobble into the adjoining dining room. The child sang and screamed without the usual reprimand he would have received had he been in his own home.

I caught Mother's pale-blue eyes fixed intently upon me. Our eyes met for a moment, enough time for me to notice her unexpressed compassion. Compassion for what? Did she know more about my life than I cared to reveal?

A quick smile came to her face as she bent over the trousers she was mending. Did this brief unspoken exchange between us signify that she might be aware of me as a human being, the first indication that perhaps she had found something in me she could like?

I went on reading but sensed her eyes resting on me. I didn't look up, afraid to risk the loss of her attention. I filled the long silence with all the words I yearned to hear from her, all the things I would have liked to tell her, but somehow could not bring myself to say. I hoped that she would speak first, create an atmosphere which could make it easy for me to express my wish for a better understanding between us; then I could confide my innermost thoughts, emotions, disappointments and strivings. I had never done this before but things had changed; something had been going on between us for a whole year, and now that we were alone I waited eagerly for a moment of communion with her.

However, Blume came home and the spell was broken.

Mother's eyes shone with pleasure as she looked at Blume's narrow face, whose large gray-green eyes were shadowed with long black eyelashes. Blume's thin lips under an upturned nose gave her a striking resemblance to Mother, though my sister was better looking. Like Mother, she smiled faintly at me. "I was at the movies. But if I'd known you were coming, I'd have stayed home," she said, and I wondered whether her words were more than politeness.

Usually, events even more important than a sister's visit wouldn't keep any of us from going to the movie which came to Niemirov for one evening, only three to five times yearly.

Guided by Bruno's childish prattling, she walked toward the dining room, opened her arms for him and carried him back to the living room.

"Put him down," Mother said. "You're too small to carry such a big boy."

Blume's frame was small and her sixteen-year-old body was still in a state of adolescence. Mother's anxiety over Blume's health had increased since Alexander's death; her care ran my sister's life smoothly without too many complications. Besides, Blume never contradicted our parents. She followed their guidelines, their orders, even their slightest suggestions.

"Bruno is so thin, he doesn't eat too well," I said.

"No, he's really quite heavy. He's only a year older than Lisa and look at the difference," Blume said. Obediently she let the child slip out of her arms and began to relate the sentimental love story she had seen on the screen, shedding a tear or two for the heroine who wasn't getting her man.

Assuming that Blume had gone with Mother's consent only, I hushed her when Father entered the house. However, she went on with her story, unperturbed to the very end.

Later, as she was walking me home, I asked her if Father knew that she went to the movies.

"Of course he knew," she said as if it were the most natural thing in the world.

He had never permitted any of us children to go to the theater or the movies. Perhaps my constant clamor for freedom to act as one pleased, freedom to disregard Orthodox rules, freedom for girls as well as for boys, had at last dented Father's impenetrable blanket of restrictions? Blume was five years younger. Had this stretch of time helped change his mind a little?

"Really, with his permission?" I asked. "Remember the guest appearance of Diana Blumenfeld, the singer I liked so much? It was almost like a holiday had been declared in town when she and her husband Jonas Turkow came to Niemirov. Everybody went to see them, only I had to steal out of the house and change my dress in Ethel's in order to go."

"You never knew how to handle Father. You always antagonized him."

"How do you manage?"

"I know I can't lure him to my world, so I *pretend* to join his. That's all."

"I don't understand. Give me an example."

"For instance: If Father wants me to say the morning and evening prayers, I don't rebel, as you always did. You reproached him for being old-fashioned. I just move my lips to give the impression that I'm praying. Father is convinced that I'm following in his footsteps and that his teachings are so strongly implanted in me that he can take more risks with me. He believes that I can withstand challenges against his way of life, so occasionally he gives me permission to do things."

I put down Bruno, whom I was carrying in my arms, and stared at Blume as if seeing her for the first time. Was this my meek little sister? Pretending so well that not only Father but I, too, had not seen through her? In the light of the new moon, and of the thousands of stars spread in the firmament, I could see her faint smile, not the color of her eyes but her dreamy look.

I could never bring myself to say something against my true convictions just to gain some benefits. Besides, I couldn't give up my right to oppose. "I didn't want our parents' love won by pretense," I said. But inside I had to admit that she saved Father and herself a lot of grief.

"That's why you had to suffer. That's why you're the 'Black Sheep' in the family."

This was news to me.

I wondered whether she was repeating a comment someone else had made or whether it was her own perception. But since my inquiry might corner her into admitting that she had branded me with a nickname, I was embarrassed to ask her.

"Here we part," I said as we reached the point of the Market Place which led to Rava-Ruska Street.

But we did not part yet. We heard voices of a few Jews coming from another side street, singing, reciting Bible quotations in a ceremony of sanctification of the new moon. We stopped and could distinguish Father's baritone among them.

"I didn't know Father went out again," Blume said. "He won't be home for a while, so I'm not in a hurry to return home. Anyway, Mother will back me up—she always does. I'll walk with you to Henia Lefkovicz's house, to play dominoes with her."

# 12

*A quarrel is like an itch:
the more you scratch, the more it itches.*

*Hasidic saying*

All the while I was helping Bruno climb the stairs I was amazed at my new insight into Blume's thinking.

We entered through the kitchen and I noticed that the door joining the kitchen with the living room, usually closed, was ajar.

Mark was sitting at the table in the center of the room reading. I had not expected him home so early. He played bridge every Tuesday evening at the home of his friend, the Polish judge, usually returning around eleven o'clock when Bruno and sometimes I were already in bed.

I took off my coat, my boots, and Xenia our housekeeper helped Bruno out of his winter clothing.

I laid my hand gently on Bruno's head and asked him to go say good night to Daddy.

"Must I?" The child looked pleadingly at me. "Go ahead, Darling, do as Mummy says." I pushed the little fellow through the half-opened door and followed him inside.

Mark took no notice of us.

"You're early tonight," I said.

"But you're late." Mark addressed me without looking up from his lawbook. "Where were you so late?"

"It's only nine o'clock," I replied and noticed Bruno stealing back to the kitchen. "Xenia," I called to the housekeeper, "please, undress Bruno and put him to bed."

"It's about time," Mark said. Then in a sharper tone of voice: "You didn't answer me. Where were you so late?"

Resenting his condescending tone of voice I raised my own. "Do you really want me to account for every step I take?"

"For every step, you say. I'm asking you where you've been with a two-year-old child late at night."

"You know where we've been."

"I don't. You tell me." He turned another page of his thick book and finally looked up at me.

"We've been at my parents," I said.

"Didn't I tell you never to go there?"

"I didn't think for a moment that you really meant it."

"I meant it and you know it. And so that there will be no doubt in your mind, I'm telling you again: I do not want you to visit your parents."

"I'll visit them anyway—" I snapped.

"If you insist on maintaining ties with those Hasidim, go ahead. But you mustn't take the child along. I'll never tolerate my son's exposure to their influence."

A slight stuttering blurred his last sentence, a sign that he was growing increasingly angry. I knew that I should keep quiet, but my hurt went too deep to do so. "What do you mean bad influence? My family is the most respected in town."

"Damn the town! I want my son to grow up in an atmosphere free of all religious prejudices. I want him to develop a sense of belonging to the nation into which he was born. We are Polish citizens. I want to forget my descent, I want my son to forget his—or better still, not even know it."

The idea he unfolded was not entirely strange to me. Some Jews, mostly of the younger generation, would suggest this pragmatic solution to the Jewish problem in an academic discussion. However, it was one thing to debate the matter and another to actually uproot oneself from the traditions instilled in most of us. "If all Jews everywhere assimilated and integrated," I said, "there would be no more Jews."

"Believe me, no one would register the loss."

"Perhaps you're right. But there are other people who think differently."

The Belzer *Rebbe* and his followers, including my father, believed that solutions of their personal and Jewish problems could be found through mysticism. Meditation, prayer, and waiting for the coming of the Messiah helped them not only to overcome difficulties encountered in their lives, but also to retain a tranquil disposition.

"Bruno is my child, too. I also have something to say about his upbringing," I said.

"This responsibility can't be left to you."

"Why not?"

"Obviously because your behavior, to say the least, has been shameful."

"What did I do?"

"To remind you of only one thing," he said slowly as if searching for the right words, "you—" he got up, started to pace the floor, took his gold-rimmed glasses off, wiped them nervously, gave me an icy look, put his glasses back on his nose and repeated "to remind you only of one thing, you ran away with me against your parents' will."

I was speechless. It took more than a moment to repress the surging anger in me. No longer in a restrained voice, I said: "Are you reproaching me for something I did out of love for you, and under your influence, almost three years ago?"

"A girl of good breeding would have had sufficient willpower to resist such influence."

"You incredible hypocrite!" I exploded. "You fell in love with a girl of 'low' breeding! You married her in spite of her lack of resistance. You talked me into it, me, the girl with an Orthodox background. In fact, you took me with nothing for a dowry. Nothing—that is, except for a fine honest background of talmudic scholars as ancestors."

"You have to cut your ties with those Hasidim."

"Never! And why do you refer to them in such a derogatory way? The Hasid you sneer at is my father and, though I reject his restrictions, I respect his idealism. His sect should be an example for other people because they not only preach ethics, *they live them*. Anyway, who are you to set yourself up as judge and jury? Who can tell which system of upbringing is better?"

He stopped pacing the floor, shut the book, slammed it against the table and glowered. "Pipe down. The neighbors downstairs may hear you. Perhaps your father who doesn't even speak Polish knows more than I do?"

"I didn't say that he has all the answers. But I can't see how his wisdom, his moral standards, can hurt our son."

He had picked up the book again and said: "If you cling to that kind of people, why didn't you marry one of *them*?"

"You know very well why I married you, but I'll ask you: 'Why did you marry me?' You could've chosen a girl from an assimilated home whose parents wouldn't annoy you. And you know something? You can still do it!"

"Damn it! Maybe I will! I warn you for the last time, don't take Bruno to your parents!"

A real threat lingered in his voice as his stuttering increased.

Seething, I was carried away by my anger: "It's obvious your resentment isn't at my father the Hasid, it's petty retaliation on your part. You can't forget that he rejected you, that he didn't want you for his son-in-law." The words had slipped out of my mouth. Too late I realized that nothing hurts more than being exposed. I regretted my remark also for my own sake because I would have to endure the penalty of his sulking and his silences for days to come. I rushed out of the living room and at the door the heavy lawbook flew in my direction, barely missing me. I slammed the door shut behind me.

# 13

*A man who persists can transform
faults into virtues if he but perseveres.*

**The Maggid of Dubno**

I tiptoed into Bruno's room and bent over his bed. He opened his round eyes and stretched his slender arms upward and around my neck. He is so frail, I thought, and rubbed his nose against my cheek as we always did before parting for the night.

"Mummy, I love you," his childish voice piped.

"I love you too," I whispered, repressing my tears. "Good night, my little bird, sleep well." I pulled the top of his pajamas down and kissed the mole on his left shoulder. Then I tucked him in and blew out the kerosene lamp.

"Mummy, please stay with me for a while," he said in a sleepy voice.

I sat down in the dark, near his bed, and thought how difficult it would be to deprive my child of his visits to his grandparents. He was so isolated in a home where no one dropped in because his father didn't like unannounced visitors. The small rented rooms on the upper floor were cramped for a growing child. He preferred my parents' spacious house, designed and built by Moshe Schall, a local contractor regarded as a genius for his excellent designs.

My parents' house was open to everyone at all times. People dropped by to read the many newspapers to which my brother

Abner subscribed. Matters of world importance and local gossip were discussed among the members of my family and the many visitors who came to see them.

Even the wandering beggars who were called *Orchim* (guests) so as not to humiliate them, were shown to the *shul*, and if they were hungry, to Lejzor Brand's house. They would get a hot glass of tea or coffee and some kind of nourishment, depending upon the time of the day and what was cooking on the stove. Father served as counsel to the Jewish as well as to the Polish town administration. He was often called upon by the local people to arbitrate their business quarrels.

Why couldn't Mark learn to respect him? His hostility never decreased in the slightest. Perhaps it had been a wrong move to open a law office in Niemirov.

It would also have been difficult to deprive myself of visits to my mother. Especially now, when I felt I was making headway in breaking down the barrier that had existed between us.

Above all, I had made progress in ridding Mark of his outmoded attitude and treatment of women. By forbidding, permitting, criticizing, he acted as if he were some kind of potentate. It reminded me that no matter how much I had tried to rid myself of the straitjacket I had been forced into by my father, I remained in a straitjacket. Only the style had changed.

I peered through the dark, through the rail of the bed, at frail Bruno peacefully asleep. His small head with his cornsilk hair rested on his arm. I recalled the sight of him right after his birth when he seemed nothing more than a piece of raw meat.

The sight had offended me so much that I had closed my eyes, crying: "Take him away, take him away."

The nurse took my baby away.

Only when I looked at my son three days later, with Mark's arm around my neck, did I see a tiny helpless being, needing me, and my heart dissolved.

Bruno was born in Lvov in the Vita Sanitarium, owned by Dr. Schwartz and Albin. I went there before delivery date after learning that my mother refused to stay at my bedside as was the custom because she wouldn't leave her textile store.

Later, she sandwiched her visits with me in the Sanitarium between her shopping expeditions for yard goods.

I felt personally rejected as I had in other circumstances in the past. However, I continued to admire her, remembering her boundless devotion to her sick, now dead, son Alexander. I recalled her carrying the rickety boy from one doctor to another, and when the medical profession gave her no hope, turning to the miracle *Rebbe* of Belz, hoping for the gift of recovery from God through his messenger the Tzaddik. Mother had spared nothing to make life bearable for her sick son.

I am luckier, I thought. I have a healthy son and I have an additional advantage: I have never been burdened by inhibitions of manifesting my true feelings for my child. And Bruno, too, expressed his feelings freely. Each time I heard the words, "Mummy, I love you," I derived new pleasure. One more glance in his direction and I felt serene.

Suddenly a thought crossed my mind.

Neither as a child, nor as an adult, had I told my mother that I loved her. Never had I indicated that I had any misgivings about her lack of affection for me. How could she know what had been in my mind, what longing there was in my heart through the years? How could one blame only Mother for our miserable relationship? Wasn't I equally to blame?

What a discovery!

I must do something about it. I must do something about it now! I must rush to Mother this very night. I must admit to her that it was my fault, too, and confess to her my difficulties with Mark. Sharing my trouble, which nobody else knew, would certainly prove to her my change of heart. Never in my twenty-one years had I talked to her of intimate matters. My confession alone would turn into the beginning of a better understanding.

Excited about my revelation, and full of hope, I pulled the blanket up over sleeping Bruno and intended to go to Mother at once.

But then I wavered. I restrained my urge and I postponed my visit.

I promised myself that I would steal out of the house the following Tuesday, when Mark would be playing bridge again.

I was plainly afraid of Mark, and I hated myself for it. I realized that I had tried to liberate myself from Father's restrictions and that I had fallen victim to Mark's.

I tiptoed out of Bruno's room and into the master bedroom. Mark was already in bed. Not to disturb him, I quietly slipped under the blanket and curled up at the very edge of the bed. But Mark was not asleep. He pulled me closer, took me into his arms and started to make love to me.

How could he kiss me? How could he caress me an hour after we had insulted each other? I felt embarrassed and wished to turn away. On second thought, considering the consequences I would have to bear, a quarrel with perhaps more violence on his part and afterwards many days of sulkiness—I let it be.

Did Bruno overhear his parents fighting? He avoided his father. He would not welcome him upon his return from the office as he used to. I felt a tender pity for Mark whenever he had to trick his son into his arms. After coming home, he usually took off his glasses, blew at the lenses, wiped them, put them back on his shapely nose and displayed a fire engine, a set of miniature dental instruments, or some candy. Bruno slowly headed in the direction of the toy but turned on his heels as soon as his father attempted to reach out for him.

He would come running to me.

"Darling, why don't you show your drawings to Daddy?" I said. "You know, Daddy, Bruno is very good at drawing!"

Bruno gathered up the loose sheets from the floor and again headed toward Mark who had the toy displayed in his hands. Mark quickly took hold of the small body on his lap and buried his face in Bruno's hair.

Sitting stiffly, the child busied himself with the new toy but slipped out of his father's embrace when the first moment presented itself.

Once he saw tears in my eyes. "Mummy, did Daddy hit you?" he asked.

"Daddy never hit your mother! Why do you ask such a question? He never hit you, did he?"

"Yes, he did so, too."

"That isn't true."

"It is. I saw him push you, and he hit my *popo*."

"Perhaps he pushed me out of the way because he was late for court, but it didn't hurt. He never hurt me. Tell me, Darling, when Daddy slapped your *popo*, was it a joke or were you a bad boy?"

"I was a bad..."

"You see," I said stroking his silken hair. I decided to demand that Mark control his temper, at least where the child was concerned.

# 14

*The man of today is a homeless, drunken mercenary,
who could be hired for the vulgar
as well as for the sublime.*

Albert Schweitzer

Though I had been able to capture my mother's attention for only a few seconds, they had become a source of strange fulfillment. I waited impatiently for Tuesday when Mark would go to his bridge party. I put Bruno to sleep, slipped into my fur coat and snowshoes, and told Xenia that I was going for a walk. I was prepared to accept the consequences if Mark discovered that I had ignored his wish.

Mother was alone. She politely asked me to sit down. "No, not there, come closer, Roma," she said and picked up the black sock she was knitting.

I pulled the chair closer, almost close enough to touch her knee. I noticed her swollen nose and red-rimmed eyes, but dared not ask her any questions, fearing that she would tell me to mind my own business as she had done many times in the past. I thought of the confession I intended to make and tried to find the right beginning. "Mother," I started, swallowed, but couldn't go on.

"You want to know why I was crying?"

"Yes... that's what I wanted to ask you."

"Today is the eighth anniversary of my mother's death. I was at the cemetery."

That, of course explained everything. One went to the grave of an ancestor to ask the deceased to intervene with God for all the things one wished to happen. For some reason it was believed that the dead were nearer to Him than were the living. One cried and lamented and asked to be forgiven for the sins one had committed, and for blessings for the future undertakings.

"I can hardly remember Grandmother Ruchel," I said.

"She was a beautiful woman," Mother said. "Warm, too, and goodhearted. Her intuitive wisdom saved us from much hardship. It was Grandmother Ruchel who urged the family to leave Poland when the First World War started in 1914. She insisted that Vienna would be the safest place for us simply because Kaiser Franz Joseph lived there. According to her, certainly no military action would ever take place near the sacred person of the Kaiser. Eventually Father yielded to her persistence. He took all of us, including Mother, to Vienna. You and the twins were not yet born.

"Restless as she was, she went out shopping for groceries before we had finished unpacking and was soon hopelessly lost. She couldn't find her way back to the grocery store, nor back home. Bewildered, she approached two women standing in a doorway and asked: 'Could you tell me where I live?'

"The women stared at her. But a second glance at your grandmother told them that she was harmless, a foreigner, and evidently in need of help. They asked her for her address. With tears in her eyes, she told them her life story but couldn't tell them her address. She had never needed to remember addresses in Niemirov.

" 'Don't worry,' one of the women said. 'You just come with us.' They reasoned that your grandmother lived in the neighborhood. On the way to the police precinct, they asked every passerby whether they knew the foreigner. One was positive that she had seen a foreign family unloading baggage across the street. She particularly recalled seeing a beautiful old lady. The stranger pointed to an apartment building on Schöngasse. Your grandmother was led to it and she was home."

It was so extraordinary for my mother to reveal something of her past, to me of all people, that I restrained my urge to laugh out loud and tried to conceal any emotion.

"She came upstairs very excited," Mother went on, "and told

us of her experience with zest and amusement. 'Not only am I well known by old and young in Niemirov, I'm just as well known in Vienna,' she said. Nevertheless, she didn't venture out alone for weeks. When she finally decided to see Vienna, it was in the company of Anna. Mother marveled at the vastness of the city and felt no bigger than a drop in an ocean, but she was not in the least discouraged. After all, she was in the same city where Kaiser Franz Josef of Austria, King of Hungary and Poland, resided, and she felt that his faithful subjects would definitely not allow the enemy to come anywhere near him. And you know something, she was right. War activities never reached Vienna."

The sock mother was knitting rested in her lap, but her hands still held onto the long needles as she chuckled while recreating the scene of Grandmother Lost in Vienna.

I, too, started to smile. "Why did you come back to Niemirov?" I asked.

"What do you mean, why did we come back. Poland is our country. All our people were born and reared here. Didn't you see our *Yichus Brief* (family tree)?"

I nodded. Of course, I had seen the parchment with many lines and names tracing our family back to 1313. Sometimes Father took it out in order to establish the degree of a relationship to one or another cousin.

"Besides," my mother went on, "we left all our relatives here and the source of your father's livelihood. There were quarries and forests which we wanted to reclaim after the war was over. There had never been any question in our hearts as to where we belonged. But coming back to Grandmother Ruchel. She was naive, but she charmed everybody, unlike myself."

"You have other qualities."

"Since early childhood, I've heard that sort of remark," she said. "Whenever your grandmother introduced me to grownups, I saw surprise in their faces and I heard sympathy in their voices when they said: 'Children change a lot while they grow.' They were wrong. I didn't change. I mean my looks didn't. Again, they would say: 'My, my, there is absolutely no resemblance between you and your daughter!' My mother would reply, 'But she's smart,' which I resented deeply. Why, this was like an admission on her part that I was homely. Many a time I was tempted to take a walk with her, but I imagined looks flitting from Mother to me, comparing and sympathizing. I pretended to have a headache, or offered to stay home with my little brother Daniel."

Her voice had trailed off to a whisper as if she were talking to herself, with no one around. Then she picked up her sock again and started to knit with such speed, as if first prize in a competition were at stake.

That my mother cared about her appearance was a revelation to me. Her untidiness and complete lack of desire for new dresses had been a source of constant irritation to me. Another revelation was her sensitivity, which surprised me because I had never suspected it in her.

I, too, must have hurt her a thousand times.

I recalled an incident that had occurred when I was twelve years old. I had always admired my friend Ethel's dresses which came from the United States. The weave of the fabric, the buttons, the buckles and the styles conveyed a world of glamor to me, the likes of which I'd never seen elsewhere. Visiting my friend during the Passover holidays, I was wearing my new dress made of a fine woolen fabric. Ethel wore a silk creation that she had put together from parts of two separate dresses out of the parcel she had received from her uncle who had emigrated to America. In no time we swapped dresses. At home, Mother gave me hell.

"A secondhand dress for a new one? And where do you think you'll wear a silk party dress? Anybody can make a fool of you!"

"I wanted this dress!"

"Get out of my way until you have your own dress back."

The humiliation as a result of retracting the deal with Ethel, coupled with the sorrow of parting with an American dress, was too much for me. "I hate you, I hate you!" I had bitterly shouted.

She had given me a peculiar glance, and her pale blue eyes filled with tears. Good, I thought. For once let her know how it feels to be despised.

That day I noticed her face repeatedly turning away from me in an attempt to hide her tears. She must have cared, it came to me, otherwise she would not have cried. Other incidents which must have been a source of hurt to her raced through my mind. Each time a friend of mine mentioned that I didn't resemble my mother, I eagerly agreed. And as if this were not enough, I hastened to emphasize that there was no inner resemblance either. Mother usually made a remark of her own: "She's the image of her Grandmother Ruchel." Like lightning, it struck me now, that Mother had avoided taking walks with me.

Watching the extraordinary speed with which she worked on the black sock, I asked: "Did I inherit the naivete of Grandmother Ruchel?"

"In a way. Oh, look what happened!—and the sock was almost finished."

A whole row of stitches had slipped off the needle and she started to pick up the first loop.

"Mother, let me help you," I said, words I'd never spoken.

She quickly looked at me and time was suspended. At that moment I felt for the first time as if I were cuddled and warmly embraced by my mother. I wished to remain alone with her a little longer. Perhaps we would finally come out into the open with our emotions.

But suddenly the door opened and a state official entered unannounced. He was a physician, employed by the district of Rava-Ruska. It was his job to check sanitary conditions in Niemirov every two weeks. The Jewish shopkeepers, in constant fear of fines, treated him royally offering him drinks and snacks. By evening, after he had made the rounds, he usually was in high spirits.

"Who is this girl?" he asked. "I never saw her before. Aren't you going to introduce us, Mrs. Brand?"

Mother, obviously displeased with the interruption, stood up, put away her knitting and said: "You've really never met her? It's my daughter, Roma. Can I help you?"

"Yes. I'd like to have a drink—served by your daughter, if you don't mind."

"Roma, see that the gentleman has a drink," mother said in a resigned voice.

From the buffet in the dining room I located a bottle of vodka, poured some into a glass and served it to him.

Glass in hand, he said: "I'm not a shoemaker, to drink by myself." Looking at me flirtatiously, he added: "Please fill another glass and drink with me."

Furious about his intrusion, I did not try to be polite. "Thank you, but I don't drink."

"You will, with me," he said firmly.

"All right, all right," Mother intervened. "She'll have a drink with you." Mother brought another glass, poured some wine and gave it to me.

The official pointed to the table standing in the center of the dining room and said, "Let's sit down and have a chat."

"I'm sorry, I must go. My husband is waiting for me."

"Husband? Is that true, Mrs. Brand? She looks so young."

"My daughter is married."

"Well, well. That's even better than I thought. An affair with a married woman suits me better than with a single girl."

"Get out of here!" I screamed, as I could no longer tolerate his flagrant abuse.

"May there be a plague to rid *our* Poland of all Jews! You, young chit, don't you ever talk back to a Polish official!" he yelled. Then he muttered some insults about the well-known modesty of Jewish women.

Mother nudged my arm, pleading with me to disregard his insults. She tried to mollify the rising excitement of the official by urging him to drink the vodka.

He jerked away from her and her red-rimmed eyes wandered from him to me and back to him as he continued to shout and gesticulate.

"You call yourself an official, you should be ashamed of yourself!" I shouted back.

Wringing her hands, Mother broke in desperately: "*Panie* (Sir), please forgive my daughter. She shouldn't talk this way, but you can see for yourself, she's *smarkata* (snotty). Roma, please—" Her eyes asked me to forgive her for calling me names.

"I'll break her! A Jewess, and she dares to defy everybody. I'll break her!"

Mother watched him now, more frightened the more he raged. As he raised his arm against me, she stepped between us, just in time to save me from the blow. His hand struck her, she screamed in pain and collapsed.

With my support, she dragged herself to her bedroom and slumped into the high bedding.

I ran for help.

Passing the official in the living room I heard him mumble something about Mother shamming sickness in order to get rid of him. Father arrived and both of us rushed to Mother, whom we found in a twisted position, moaning.

He lay down beside her and took her gently into his arms. The palm of his hand pressing against her forehead, he asked in a sweet voice I had never heard before: "How do you feel, my dear? Where does it hurt?"

Mother sighed, drew closer to him, but said not a word.

I had never before thought of them as two people in love. They had never once displayed any emotion in front of their children. To me it had been a partnership devoted to a single purpose: the fulfillment of their parental duties and responsibilities.

Mother sat up in an obvious effort to catch her breath.

Father, pale, hunched over her, called her pet names. He tried to help her find a more comfortable position. I took two pillows from the other bed and placed them under Mother's head. She looked at me lovingly but said nothing. Then I left the bedroom, angry with myself. The blow intended for me had struck Mother.

The official was telling neighbors who had gathered that Mrs. Brand was pretending to be hurt because he had raised his arm in a joking gesture and had "accidentally" brushed her chest. At this point Father scolded me from a distance for standing around. "Run for a doctor, Roma, run!"

I rushed to the only drugstore in town. The druggist's daughter had married a physician and lived with her parents in their own house on Rava-Ruska Street. Though my words to the doctor were incoherent, he took his coat and bag, leaving his tea untouched. Turning back at the door, he pulled his wife's coat out of a closet and threw it over my shoulders.

Mother, in a contorted position, was struggling to catch her breath. Desperately Father tried to calm her. He supported her back when she sat up and adjusted the pillows when she lay down. He wiped the perspiration from her forehead, dipped his hand in a bowl of cold water and pressed his palm against Mother's forehead. How well I knew this procedure. Each time his moistened hand touched her face she sighed with relief. Then she groaned and Father took her in his arms.

The doctor opened his bag. he took out a needle. He filled it with a liquid and stepped up to the bed. He took Mother's arm.

He didn't give her the prepared injection. He felt her pulse and hesitated. He grew pale.

"How is she, doctor?" I asked. "How is she?"

He shrugged.

Mother appeared to be dozing peacefully in Father's arms. He rocked her, very gently, his eyes blank, staring at the white wall before him.

I couldn't understand why the doctor put the needle back into his case and why he reached for his coat and his wife's coat. Grasping his lapels, I begged, "Please don't go. Please, Doctor, help *my mother*!"

The doctor looked wistfully at me and placed his hands on my shoulders. "No further help is needed. Your mother is free of pain."

Shaking my shoulders free of his hands, I said, "Don't refuse. She needs you!"

"You don't understand!"

"It's not true! This can't be true!" Half way to the bed he caught me and pulled me out of the room. I couldn't tear my gaze away from Father who rocked my mother from side to side, from side to side.

The funeral took place the following day.

We walked from our house toward Jaworow Street, ankles deep in snow. The outskirts of the town seemed covered by a clean starched sheet. At the cemetery, we saw a path in the snow which the grave diggers had made. It led to the pit waiting to swallow Mother.

A few feet ahead of her grave some footprints frozen in the snow led to another grave, my Grandmother Ruchel's grave. The footprints were Mother's who had been to the cemetery the day before, the day of her mother's eighth *Jahrzeit* (Anniversary of death).

I sobbed out my grief, carrying on interminable silent conversations with my mother, telling her all the things I had never told her while she was alive. During the long hours and days when each member of the family was wrapped in grief, I mourned alone.

My loss was the most severe. For the first time she had revealed herself to me, to nobody but me. It had filled me with joy that she had opened the gate to her heart. Only once before in my whole life did I experience this kind of joy, the moment when I gave birth to Bruno. There was the sudden sense of relief from pain and exhilaration upon hearing the baby's cry. I knew now I had won Mother's love. But I let the blow, intended for me, strike her. I felt that after years of gestation I had succeeded in giving birth to her love. Then I felt that Mother had delivered me for the second time and had died at childbirth. My mind was blurred, our roles changed and changed. I conceived her and then again I was her daughter. Regardless of the transformation, one thing was certain; something new, something beautiful, had been created and irretrievably lost. I was without it. She, who had just given me what I had yearned for all my life, was no more.

# 15

*Unconcerned about the means, the villains are always more pragmatic and expedient.*

*Franz Grillparzer*

Bruno was with me in the textile store playing with Lisa when I happened to look out of the window and saw the official from the Sanitation Department heading in our direction. I wondered whether he would, at least this time, pass us by and enter the grocery store next door. His green breeches neatly tucked into his high, polished boots, his brown leather jacket unbuttoned, he hesitated for a split second before entering our store.

Upon noticing me, he was unable to hide his uneasiness. He slowly closed the door, probably to gain time weighing what course of action to take. He said, "Good afternoon," and doffed his checkered sport cap, which he seldom did. Crushing it clumsily in his hand, he moved forward. As Abner took it from him and placed it on the counter, he seemed relieved. Anyway, he had regained his composure.

Abner's courtesy irritated me. Only six weeks had passed since Mother's death. Had Abner forgotten that this man had caused it?

The official walked briskly from one corner of the store to the other, stopping here and there, looking, shaking his head in disapproval and finally verbally criticizing:

"The spittoon is not placed in the right spot."

Abner pushed the enamel basin with his foot to where the official had pointed.

I sensed that Abner's submissiveness encouraged the official to be his old boisterous self. I sent a message to Abner with my eyes and hoped he would understand.

"Children must not run around in the store," the official said.

"Were my mother alive, neither I nor my brother would have to help out and there would be no children in the store," I remarked embittered.

"Please, Roma," Abner whispered in Yiddish. "Control yourself, they're our masters."

The official found fault with the clock. We had more than once been reminded by the local Police of the regulations designating a certain place for the spittoon, a specific color for the garden and yard fences and so on. But, I had never heard of any legislation regarding a fast- or slow-running clock.

This official was once again harassing us.

I asked him through my teeth: "What time should it be now, according to *your* law?"

Disregarding my sarcasm, he looked at his wristwatch: "Two o'clock sharp," he said. "Orders are to be obeyed!"

Abner asked Bruno to get out of his way, climbed obediently up on a chair to adjust the clock hanging high over the doorpost.

"Idiot!" I drawled through my teeth at Abner. And listening to my heart and not to my reason I said to the official: "If there would be some order, you would be behind bars instead of annoying people who have not yet recovered from the tragedy *you* brought upon them."

"Shut up, *zydowa* (kike)!"

I slapped him full in his face.

There was complete silence.

Then he screamed: "To hell with you all! A crazy family!" He grabbed his cap and cussing some more, he left.

"You are truly crazy, Roma! You're asking for trouble, and Lord knows you'll get it!"

Too well did I fear that Abner was right. I was scared, mostly of Mark's reproaches, but somehow I had no regrets. How much abuse was my brother willing to take? I gave that official what he deserved.

"You think you're the only proud one among us. We have pride, too, but we know we'll never win, that's why we have to control ourselves. And we do. Wait till Father hears about it."

"It's no use," Father said. "They have the upper hand, we cannot make things easier than they are, so a little humility, my child, would be more fitting."

Each separately and together reprimanded me. All of them looked gloomily into the future. And they were right. The official filed suit against me for hampering him in executing his duties and for insulting him while performing them.

At the hearing in court, I was calm, for I had a plan. Disregarding Mark's instructions only to answer the judge's questions, to keep the answers short and precise, I requested permission to tell the story my own way.

I noticed Mark removing his eyeglasses, wiping them long enough to know he was angry with me. I concentrated on the judge's double chin while telling him of the circumstances leading to my mother's death. Mark twice made an attempt to interrupt me. However, the judge, with a sympathetic smile on his good-natured face, insisted that I go on.

I could hardly believe my ears when the judge advised me through Mark to take my complaint to the Criminal Court in a separate action. When he went on to say that this was an administrative suit and was to be handled without consideration of the circumstances pertaining to my mother's death, Mark nodded agreeably.

"Did you strike the official while he was inspecting your parents' store?"

"But—"

"Yes? or no?"

"Yes."

I was sentenced to five days in prison.

"I told you," Mark reprimanded me on the way home, "to leave the talking to me. You made a fool of me. As the wife of an attorney, you should know better. It was as if I hadn't instructed you in advance."

I did not answer. Had not the world of justice in which I had been reared crumbled suddenly in this court which I had just left? Was it possible that the one who caused the death of a human being might go scot free while another who merely hit the scoundrel be imprisoned?

Mark's needling penetrated my mind slowly. "Do you see, what a mess you got yourself into by not listening to me, by insisting on remaining friendly with your relatives? It's a good thing that you have me to look after you."

If he really were concerned about me, would he be squabbling about things he could never change, I thought. I preferred to be left alone.

He took my arm, "Don't worry, Roma, you'll not go to prison. I'm going to appeal the case."

I was not concerned about prison at all. My thoughts went back to my mother's funeral, which Father had arranged hastily in fear that the authorities, considering the circumstances of her death, might insist upon an autopsy.

And now, to file a countersuit against the official was for the same reason unthinkable. To Father, an autopsy would mean desecration of the corpse. He would never permit such a thing.

"Would you file suit against the official if it were solely up to you?" I asked Mark.

"Of course, I would!"

I snuggled up to him and walked home with a feeling of such comfort that in spite of everything, my husband had more strength of character than my relatives. Or so it seemed to me at least on that point.

One year later Father married Perele, a young woman who had been married twice before and divorced because she had remained childless. Treasuring her dream, she hoped to have it fulfilled by her third husband, father of six children. Each month when she saw her hopes crushed, her almond-shaped, black eyes filled with tears and she became moody and irritable. Her beautiful face of a peachy complexion, framed by jet-black hair mostly covered by a kerchief, became flushed. She hardly spoke to anybody.

The depression lasted only a few days. We children never complained to Father about the difficulties we had with his wife. No doubt she was aware of our consideration for as time passed a fine relationship of mutual loyalty and trust developed and deepened between us.

# 16

*In everyone there is something precious, found in no one else;
so honor each man for what is hidden within him—
for what he alone has and none of his fellows.*

*Hasidic saying*

Not until a German newpaper falsely accused Poland of sending troops which attacked a radio station in Kleiwitz did anybody pay attention to the rumors of an approaching war. September 1, 1939, the Germans started the war.

Few people subscribed to the daily newspapers. Most of the Niemirovers received news on street corners. A policeman beat the drums long enough to have people come out of their stores and houses. When enough gathered he stopped drumming and in a loud voice he communicated new rules and orders.

That's how every young man found out about the draft into the Polish Army. The verbal announcement in this particular case was followed by a letter from the Military.

Each drafted Pole boasted that his physical strength combined with his hatred for the enemy would enable him to stand up against ten Germans.

The Ukrainians welcomed any Polish entanglement. This might give them an opportunity to make deals with the Germans and to establish an autonomy of their own with Lvov as their capital.

The Jews, a disliked minority under Polish rule, were fearful of every new regime.

Among many Jews hurriedly drafted in Neimirov was Benny the bookbinder. Tall and husky, he could tear a book in two without any visible effort. Wherever there was a brawl, Benny's appearance put an end to it. Each of the parties involved preferred to be beaten by his opponent than by Benny. Often, without lifting his powerful arm, he became the peacemaker.

Once he was drafted, his mother, a frail little woman who always ordered him around, followed him in silence. She came with him into our textile store to choose some foot-wrappings. While touching this and that fabric, she offered him loving advice on how to take care of himself and how to avoid brawls. "Here you are the Hercules. There, among a million Goyim, you'll not be the giant. Don't show your strength, play it down, Bennele, otherwise they'll gang up against you and kill you." She seemed less afraid of the German enemy than of her own countrymen.

"Stop worrying so much," my stepmother Perele said. "Look at Hanna's Jankiel. *Nebbich* a sickly boy, all he knows is how to study Talmud. Him they shouldn't have taken."

"Actually we should be proud that we're going to serve," Benny said.

His mother and Perele looked at him in surprise. To them this was heresy on Benny's part. How could one go to kill without feeling revulsion? "Why?" his mother asked.

"Because finally we've reached equality. We always knew that we were Polish citizens but the Poles didn't want us. Now they need us. Now they treat us the way we always wanted to be treated. Now they can't call me *parszywy zyd* (dirty Jew)."

"So for that he has to give his life?" his mother cried.

"*Mamenew*, many soldiers come back from battle, not everybody gives his life."

"He thinks if he reads books, he knows it all."

"Is reading books a crime?"

"Not if you'd read holy books. Then you'd give your old mother more respect. My heart is on fire and he speaks of books."

"Mother," Benny seemed exasperated, "Mother, let's pay for the wrappings and go. We still have a lot of things to do."

"Bennele, listen to your mother and let's buy the sweater we saw in Abe Klager's store, please."

"But, Mother, there will be no money left for you," I heard him whisper as they went to the exit.

Her olive skin flushed red, Perele put the three zlotys into the drawer serving as cash register. Tears veiled her expressive black eyes. Those tears, were they shed in sympathy for Benny, or for his mother? "He talks nonsense," she said to me after the two were gone. "What equality do we get? Cannon-fodder equality. Is that what he wants, the poor slob? How many mothers will see their sons again? Which of them will receive the brief notice that her son died a hero's death?"

Her bitterness over all her barren years had melted. She, the childless woman, was now spared the worry, the frustration of the waiting. Then, embarrassed by her own momentary relief, she started to cry for all of the sons.

"Look, Roma, here is Berely Ferber, Mayer Schall, and there is—what's his name?—Schwartz. Too bad he didn't make it in time to England like his redhead brother. Look how pale he is." She blew her nose, wiped her tears and added: "And there is Baruch Reich. All of them will be drafted. I dread this miserable thought."

If there was misery, it was not visible to me. Self-confident, the boys marched shoulder to shoulder, their boots shining and their faces, too. Proudly their women looked on. Benny's marching in his Polish uniform among the Poles, chest out, stomach in, elevated to a dignity he never knew before, made him forget the dangers ahead, at least during the time of parading and being cheered by the onlookers. Only when he heard his mother calling after him, he turned helplessly to catch another glimpse of her. Now he seemed to be a little boy in need of a kiss or of a pat on his shoulder. He seemed in need of a word or two approving of his action, although he had no choice anyway. His mother caught up with him, marched alongside him, but could not keep up with the soldiers' stride and fell breathlessly behind. She kept calling after him.

Benny's shoulders, visible above the heads of the soldiers behind him, suddenly sagged. I wouldn't have been surprised if Benny were weeping.

The march of the Polish troops to the front at the end of the summer in the year 1939 was on the whole an inspiring sight. Self-confidence emanated from almost all of them. The soldiers wore their caps jauntily and sang songs of courage and love as they moved forward in the brilliant sunshine, leaving a cloud of dust behind.

Women, children and older men lined both sides of the streets. Some of the spectators held their heads proudly, others had tears in their eyes. One Pole called out the name of a passing husband, another of a son, or father. Their voices were drowned by the soldiers' swelling song:

> *"Moja pierwsza brygada*
> *strzelecka gromada*
> *na stos rzucilismy*
> *swoj zycia los*
> *swoj zycia los—"*

# 17

*Wealth doesn't consist of fortunes
but how one is using them.*

*Napoleon I*

My father approved of my suggestion to invest all his cash money in yard goods and I volunteered to go to Lvov where we customarily purchased merchandise. In the wholesale store on Rzerznicka Street, I was concerned over getting the best value in the smallest quantities and therefore selected expensive imported silks and woolens. Now the clerk displayed a piece of pure silk with a floral print. Gina, who was with me, coaxed me to take it. "The peasants in Niemirov will gobble it up, it's such a gay design," she said.

To me, the small flowers printed in varying shades of red seemed suddenly to be never-ending drops of blood. I pushed it away.

"It's only twenty meters," the clerk said. "You'll regret it if you don't take it."

My dislike of the fabric became so intense that I turned my face away and pointing at the yard goods already heaped on the counter, I said: "By now, I am out of money," and I asked him to pack my merchandise and to prepare the invoice while I would look for a dorożka or a man with a pushcart. It was then that we heard a deafening thunder.

Outside, some people were looking at the sky which stretched in an uninterrupted blue. Was it possible that a storm was coming without a single cloud in the sky?

Gina and I were looking at each other and then in the same direction other people did. We heard a faint buzzing and when the sound of the buzzing increased people dispersed within seconds. At the same time a few black specks on the sky grew larger and soon we could see planes sweeping across the sky.

Gina and I were back in the store at once and we heard another deafening roar.

The store owner, ducking behind the counter, yelled, "Down on the floor!" and pulled his clerk with him.

The first one to straighten up was Gina. "A storm is coming," she said unconvincingly, her green eyes staring through the window.

The store owner's twelve-year-old son came in with his mother. The boy ran to his father, "Daddy, Mother said that we should be together in a time like this."

His mother wrung her hands and whined, "It's the end of the world!"

Two clerks from a neighboring store came in and we found out what it was all about. The railroad station had been bombarded by the Germans and many civilians were dead, and many were wounded. One clerk had seen a truck loaded with critically wounded.

"With my own eyes I saw men with open stomachs, women with legs torn off and even mutilated children with their blood dripping to the gutters on the way to the hospital," another shopkeeper came in to tell us.

Shocked by the suddenness of the attack, our hatred for the Germans reached a boiling point as the bombardment of the city continued. Apartment houses in rubble, innocent people killed, many wounded in the hospitals, we talked of the unprecedented cruelty of our enemy and agreed that civilization would be wiped out in months if this kind of warfare was allowed to continue.

I stored the merchandise I had bought for myself with Gina in Lvov and took Father's back to Niemirov by bus, the last that was to run between the two cities.

Shortly thereafter, Polish money began to be devaluated by the hour and we knew we had made a profitable investment.

Father did not think of selling the textiles at once. He stored them partly in the cellar and partly in the home of our Gentile friend, Ivan Trusievicz, for safekeeping.

Through the radio Polish commentators fed the population with assurances that the fifteen Polish divisions were strong enough to withstand the German attack. Nevertheless, Jewish men fled from Cracow, Rzeszov and other cities near the German borders, in an attempt to escape the advancing enemy. Refugees flowed through Niemirov by car, by bus, and the less fortunate who could not hire a horse and wagon came on bicycles.

An acquaintance lawyer by the name of Rosner, with three of his friends, had fled Rzeszov on bicycles leaving their wives behind, claiming that women had nothing to fear from the Germans.

I brought them to my parents who set them up for the night in their house. Rosner was in a hurry to leave next morning, but his friends argued that it would be over soon and they wanted to return back home. They had heard Marszal Rydz-Smigly assure the nation over the radio that Polish armed forces had the means to repulse all attacks, whether launched by enemies from the west or the east. They also claimed to know that our Secretary of State Beck had received new guarantees from England and France. (Beck himself was on the run to a foreign country only a few days later.) It became evident that running within Poland was useless, that the Germans were already on the heels of the fleeing and would catch up with them.

Rosner and his friends were tired and fell asleep as soon as their heads touched the pillows. Rosner and one of his buddies left next morning eastward, the other two remained in my parents' house.

Father treated them royally, as if they were honored guests. His wife Perele fed them and other refugees passing through Niemirov, wining and dining them and putting them up for the night. At first in the attic rooms and then in the living room also. When still more kept pouring in, Father spread straw on the floor, Perele took out all the sheets and blankets and accommodated as many as possible.

The 15th of September, two weeks after Hitler's Army had stepped on Polish soil as part of a concocted plot, the retreat of the Polish Army became a fact in spite of Polish radio and press releases to the contrary. After 18 days it became obvious that Poland was defeated.

Only a few weeks ago we had watched and were greatly impressed by the Polish Military Units heading westward. It had seemed only yesterday that Benny's mother had bought the foot-wrappings in our store; only yesterday that Benny, proud of his uniform, had marched away; only yesterday that the Poles boasted of being able to defeat an enemy army tenfold larger than theirs.

If a thousand soldiers had massed in Niemirov a few weeks ago, it looked as if ten thousand were returning east. The disorderly conduct of those retreating, their accelerated speed harassed and worried the local population. It became clear that they were no longer a disciplined fighting force trained to obey orders. In that short time they had become a riotous herd brutally determined to overcome every obstacle in their way to assure their safe retreat.

Father said that all soldiers on the run were the same. Abner did not know whom to fear more, our own troops or the fast advancing Germans. One day two Poles ran after him, wanted to beat him, cursing that the Jews were responsible for the war and for the retreat. Luckily, *Reb* Alter saw him from his window, opened the door at just the right moment and pulled him inside.

"It's hard to be a Jew," Father said.

"It's strange, neither will let us alone. But even blindfolded I'd vote for the Poles. It's here where we belong—"

"You mean until the coming of the Messiah," Father interrupted.

He took out the last pinch of tobacco, sniffed and sneezed.

Fat cat Tin-Tin came running and rubbed his body against Father's leg.

Bruno made believe that he was sneezing and said that he liked best of all the dwarf Sneezy.

Father and Perele offered vodka and food to the Polish soldiers who entered their home. Then they stopped serving alcoholic drinks and food for there was little left for their own family and the two Rzeszover. Later, there was none at all. Even Tin-Tin was no longer the fat cat.

Some soldiers came barefoot and in tattered rags. It was unusually warm for the middle of September and the soldiers, now mostly on foot, were exhausted, ready to collapse. Father had placed a bucket full of water in front of his house so the passing soldiers could help themselves.

Benny's mother stood nearby for hours. She expected her

son to be among the retreating. Once in a while the little woman mobilized enough courage to approach someone timidly: "I apologize, *Panie* officer," she addressed every soldier officer, "I apologize, *Panie* officer, for bothering you. You see, I, too, have a son in the Polish Army. As your mother is waiting for you, that's how I'm waiting for my Bennele. Did you perhaps see him?"

Some stared at her, some broke into laughter.

Red patches on her face, she would go on: "You could have met him, it's possible, isn't it? He's very tall, he's beautiful, he's very strong, his name is Benny and he is a bookbinder."

Some gave her a sympathetic glance and answered politely, "I'm sorry, I haven't met your son." Most did not bother to answer. Others pointed at her head implying she was crazy.

She sighed, leaned against the wall and waited for another opportunity. She waited from morning until dawn for her son's return or for some word from him.

Father's corner house, located in the Market Place where three roads crossed, was the right place for Benny's mother to seek information. But it was also one of the most exposed in town. Father started to complain of the dangers of living there. Now, even Benny's mother in her worn brown dress, too large for her small body, was scared. She stood pressed against the brown brick wall and gave the impression that she was part of the wall. Since she had been pushed and pulled and kicked a few times, the intervals between her inquiries became longer and longer.

"Come in." Perele invited her for a glass of hot tea. She believed that nothing quenched thirst better than hot tea. "Maybe he's hiding somwhere in Lubaczov," Father said to her. "Maybe he's waiting for the road to become safer. Maybe he will surprise you when you'll least expect him."

Benny's mother pulled up a chair facing a window and sitting on the edge of it, sipped tea and crushed cubes of sugar between her teeth. She did not touch the slice of bread, a luxury because it was spread with a little butter obtained by one of Father's faithful laborers, a peasant from Radroz who had brought him a gift. She continued staring out the window.

One night when Father declined to open the door, three Polish soldiers broke in. They asked for vodka. After raiding the house and not finding vodka, they went to the cellar and took some of the textiles, sterling silver candlesticks and whatever else of value they could lay their hands on. They emptied two burlap sacks of potatoes, stuffed them with the loot and carried them out without anybody daring to interfere.

They promptly exchanged the candlesticks for vodka with a Gentile and the textiles changed hands for the same price.

The next night, threatened at gunpoint, Father handed over money and some jewelry. We were happy at that because nobody was harmed.

The looting became commonplace. Plain hoodlums from neighboring villages armed themselves and took advantage of the general confusion. Dressed in stolen uniforms, they pretended to be retreating soldiers and easily got away with robbing Jews.

Since the local hoodlums "visited" the rich Jews mostly, Father moved with his family into the hut of a beggar well-known in Niemirov, where no one would expect to find anything of value. *Reb* Alter, Benny's mother, and other friends carried what was left of his yard goods piece by piece to the beggar's hut. The two refugees, Rosner's friends from Rzeszov, came along.

With the exception of my parents, everyone slept in the barn which had been empty anyway. The two Rzeszover came inside the three-room hut only at mealtimes. They were still waiting for a safe opportunity to go back home.

Father alone had the means to buy food and the beggar had the courage to walk to some village to get it. He was often seen on his return carrying a sack of flour on his back and a live chicken under his arm.

Whenever I was scared by the noise of artillery or by the buzzing of the bombers in the air, I took Bruno to the top of the hill on Radroz Street where other townspeople gathered. There we would find Father, Perele, the rest of the family and Tin-Tin. For some reason, we felt better and safer on the outskirts of the town. Perhaps we felt that our homes could not withstand a bombing.

There on the hill the members of our family separated as soon as we saw or heard a bomber in the sky. Father and Perele remained sitting under the oak tree.

Next to Bruno, Mark and I hugged the earth on the slope in the shade of a protruding rock. Tin-Tin ran from Father to Bruno and from Bruno to Father.

Benny's mother had taken a fancy to Abner and followed him like a shadow. She took care of his Lisa like a loving grandmother, making it easier for Sara who was now visiting with us on the slope. Adela and her husband settled closer to our parents. Each group was separated by only a few yards from the other. In a way we were together and the suspense of what fate had planned for us was easier to bear.

Only Mark seldom moved from where he happened to be at the time of the approaching planes. "Your father thinks he is smart, separating the family members. What does he say?" And mocking Father's baritone voice, he repeated his words: " 'If a bomb were dropped, I want at least some of you to survive so that our family tree will have a chance of growing.' He is so ignorant that he doesn't know what he is talking about."

I looked around and was relieved that nobody could hear him.

"A bomb," he went on, "costs money. Lots of money. So much money that the few people on this hill aren't worth the expenditure."

Fewer and fewer retreating Poles passed through Niemirov, until we saw only single individuals in rags hardly sufficient to cover their bodies, too beaten and weak to walk upright along the highway.

Bruno called my attention by pointing his finger at the highway below.

As far as my eyes could see, there was not a sign of life or movement. Now a motorcycle came into sight speeding over the uneven highway. A single shot pierced the air and then another. One of the two men fell to the ground and only one remained on the vehicle. The man left behind on the ground attempted to get up, but failed. Would his buddy leave him behind and run to safety by himself? I wondered very cooly.

The motorist turned his head, slowed down, made a U turn and stopped near the wounded man. He leaned his vehicle against a telephone pole and bent over his friend. He folded his friend's arms around his neck and succeeded in straightening him up. He inched step by step toward the telephone pole. Suddenly another shot pierced the air. And another. The two intertwined bodies fell and remained motionless on the ground.

# 18

*When a father helps a son, both smile;
when a son must help his father, both cry.*

*Hasidic saying*

The noise of artillery subsided and the rattling of machine guns started. Then silence and then German soldiers appeared seemingly from nowhere. Nobody saw them coming. Clean shaven, in their spotless green-gray uniforms and neat military boots, they leaped nimbly over garden gates and fences. Rifles ready to fire, they moved quickly in groups of four toward the houses.

Father under the oak, twisting his red beard, called out to us. "Let's go home and leave the rest to the Almighty."

Mark's sarcastic smile veiled by his English-style mustache irritated me.

Blume picked up the plaid blanket that had been spread on the grass and folded it.

Adela asked where Perele was and someone answered that she and Sara had remained home.

Bruno clasped his hands, his face aglow with excitement. With his index finger he pointed to the right then to the left where more and more Germans continued to appear. Now we saw small tanks rolling towards Niemirov in great numbers as if the whole German Army was on its way to proudly display its strength. Both the tank soldier on top and the infantry soldier on foot seemed fit for battle.

But they met with no opposition.

Only the Ukrainians, assuming that they would benefit from the German invasion, were on hand to give whatever information they could about local conditions. Later they were also available when a new temporary town administration was formed and they became the majority of the acting body, subordinate only to the Germans.

The first day in Niemirov, the Germans shot Duzy Hirschfeld, the chairman of the *Kultus Gemeinde* (Jewish Administration).

The highways in great need of repair were among the first urgent jobs to be taken care of under German supervision. The work had to be done by Jews. The following morning after the German invasion, four soldiers and one Ukrainian entered the beggar's hut and asked that all men of the Jewish faith step up near the door.

The beggar, Father, Abner, and one of the Rzeszover refugees followed the order. Only Ivan Trusievicz who happened to be visiting with us and the other Rzeszover refugee remained seated. The soldiers led the Jews out of the hut.

The Rzeszover who had remained seated cursed that no German son of a bitch was going to order him around and he wondered why Abner, like himself, had not resisted our enemy.

Three minutes later, one of the four soldiers came back, screamed at the top of his lungs that no Jewish swine would ever again deceive an honest German doing his job. Why hadn't he admitted that he was Jewish.

They grabbed him and threw him out of the hut.

Later he was found shot in the back of his neck on the road to Lubaczov where my family, among fifty other Jews, were working as quarriers.

Father, being a specialist in highway building, pointed out an easier way of cutting stone. He was promptly clubbed by a guard and told to mind his own business. Though he never again opened his mouth, he came home the following days with black-and-blue marks. He never complained. Compared with death, what was a little beating?

After Duzy Hirschfeld and the Rzeszover were shot the Niemirover took it as a warning and henceforth blindly obeyed

German orders. Father was ready and willing to take a bruise here and there as long as he was allowed to go home after a backbreaking day's work. "Work never killed anyone," he repeated every night. "Another few months and the war will be over. The best thing is to accept everything humbly as God wills."

Father asked me to move in with him. His argument: both families would keep one household; easier availability of food for my own family. But then he timidly admitted: "I feel safer with you around. You, Roma, speak German so well."

So in effect Father handed me an *a priori* approval for actions I might take. It was not the woman he approached, it was the *person* who spoke the German language so well and could therefore become a benefit to him. An inkling came to me of having punched at least a few holes in the traditional bag where women's rights had been kept. The achievement filled me with pride. For more reasons than that one I wanted to satisfy Father's request.

While setting the table for dinner, I said to Mark: "Today we have a treat. Guess what? Eggs, butter, and freshly baked bread. How do you like your eggs, scrambled or fried?"

"Fried, please."

"Then we'll all have fried. Mark, the whole town is in an uproar. Remember the two Rzeszover who had remained in Niemirov? One of them was shot by the Germans. First Duzy Hirschfeld and now the Rzeszover. He's lying near the arch on Lubaczov Street and the Germans don't let anyone touch the body. And you know why they killed him? Just because he didn't admit that he was Jewish. I can't believe it but it's true. *Reb* Alter is going to steal the body. He wants to take it to the cemetery and give him a Jewish funeral. He has no relatives here so Father is going to say *Kaddish* after him. Everybody who has courage is going to the funeral."

"You are not going!" Mark exclaimed.

I certainly would have, but for now I refrained from quarreling with him.

"Mummy, look, Daddy made a ship for me."

"It's a beautiful ship," I said.

The relationship between father and son had greatly improved. Mark had lots of time to spend with Bruno because his law office had been closed from the day of the German invasion. And luckily he had not been caught by the Germans and had not done work for them until now.

The white tablecloth, the flavor of the bread Perele had baked that very morning and had given me to take home, the aroma of the fried eggs, now a rare treat, with Mark and Bruno together, made me forget what was going on outside my four walls, as if our Poland had not lost the war within twenty-six days.

We had the kind of appetite one has only after sickness or when there is not enough food to be had and we ate to our heart's delight. Even Bruno's appetite had improved. Then I put Bruno to bed and Mark and I remained alone.

"Mark," I started in a soft voice, "Father asked that we move into the hut—"

"Never! Never!" he shouted and the pleasant atmosphere was shattered as if a piece of china had been violently thrown to the ground.

"Mark, please listen, Mark. It might be of great benefit to us too."

"I don't want to listen to your reasons," he interrupted. "It's no-o-o!" He took his glasses off, cleaned them furiously while pacing the floor up and down, up and down.

"Don't be so opposed to it, there is a war going on—"

"Stop it! I told you once and for all, I am not interested in your arguments. Stop it!" He had replaced his eyeglasses and used his hands to cover his ears.

"When are you moving in?" Father asked two days later when I visited him in the hut. I kept my eyes fixed on the earthen floor, embarrassed for not having complied with his S.O.S. and also for having succumbed to my husband's chauvinism.

"Mark doesn't like the idea? Never mind. But I have another favor to ask of you. Since we moved to the hut our vacant house is more apt to be looted and demolished. I'd appreciate it if you were to stay in there with Blume for a few hours daily. It'll give the impression that it's not deserted, that it is lived in."

Although I knew that Mark would be against it I agreed. This time I would assert my will!

As I expected, he called it a very risky proposition and he

refused to become a babysitter in place of Xenia who had left us.

"Do you prefer me to take Bruno along?" I threatened.

"No. I expect you to stay home with us where you belong."

Disregarding his wish I stayed in Father's house with Blume from twelve noon until four o'clock and quarreled every day with Mark before leaving and after returning.

# 19

*Groups are more immoral
than individuals.*

Aristotle

Once, while in my father's vacant house, I heard a knock on the door. It must be Henia Lefkowicz, I thought, Blume's friend, the only one who had visited with her twice before. But when the knocking became obtrusive, I knew it could not be her because, a daughter of Orthodox parents, she was brought up in modesty and humility.

I looked at Blume and she looked at me. I got up, but stood undecided until the knocking became intolerable.

"Who can it be?" Blume asked as I went to the entrance door.

Two uniformed Germans, one heavy-set, the other very thin, stood before me and asked whether this was the home of the Brand family. I nodded and the thin one pushed me aside and both entered. "We want to see Brand," the thin one said.

"I'm sorry, he's not here."

"Where is he?"

"I don't know."

"You know, and we have the means of making you tell."

"Mr. Brand is working on the highway," I lied.

"Not today. Nobody is working on the highway *today*."

How well I knew. Only an hour ago when I had gone to the beggar's hut to fetch Blume, I had seen and spoken to Father,

Abner and some Jewish neighbors. They were resting and trying to guess why they had been sent home.

The heavy-set German fixed his brown eyes on my face and said: "You know where Brand is. You bring him over. We merely want to ask him a few questions. If you don't we'll have to use force to make you."

I did not take my eyes away from his while a hundred thoughts raced through my mind. Then I took a deep breath and said, "If you give me your word as a German officer that you will not harm Mr. Brand I will try to find him."

"I give you my word," the heavy-set one said.

"Stop playing games," the thin one fumed. "Let her bring the swine at once!"

Both of them remained with Blume while I ran to the beggar's hut. What did they want of Father? What kind of questions did they want to ask? Suddenly I realized that perhaps they wanted my brother? They asked for Brand. It could just as well be *Abner* Brand. He was young, physically stronger, and more worldly. He could perhaps cope with the situation more easily than Father.

Abner's wife would not let him go. She cried, said that I should go back and tell them I could not find Brand anywhere and when Abner went along, Sara called out a warning to me that the responsibility would be mine if anything happened to her husband. And she wasn't even aware that I had made the choice between Father and Brother on my own.

There was not time to listen to her. A new worry was choking me. What if the two military men had sent me away on a false pretense to insure Blume's being alone? What if they planned to harm her? I raced back and Abner followed.

Blume was all right. I caught my breath. I introduced my brother as Brand and the heavy-set soldier took him into the dining room and closed the door behind them. The thin one remained with us.

My mind raced with fear and apprehension. What was going on behind those closed doors? Poor Sara, already distraught with my bringing Abner to the Germans, how would she react when she found out that they never specifically asked for *him*. I felt the impending guilt should adversity come to my brother.

Finally Abner came out, unharmed! I looked at him. His face was impassive but for the anxiety in his blue eyes.

The heavy-set German called me into the dining room.

The first thoughts were that he had seen through my game, that he wanted Father and that I was going to get punished for deceiving him. However, his first question pointed to a completely different area: "Where did you hide your yard goods?"

"What yard goods?"

"Don't pretend. Where did you hide them?"

"I did not."

"You did. Brand just told me that you are, in fact *the only one* who knows where the yard goods are. Tell me, we'll confiscate them, and leave you alone."

I could not control a smile. So Abner, without knowing how I tricked him into his troublesome situation for Father's sake, threw the ball right back into my lap.

The German was puzzled. "After you've shown me the hiding place, all of you will be set free," he said, implying that as of now he considered us under arrest.

"All right then, I will show it to you. It's in the house of our friend, but please, may I first explain something to you?"

He lit a cigarette and leaned against the door post.

His relaxed position somewhat inflated my courage. "We do have some yard goods," I started. "But those who gave you this information don't know that by now most of it is gone. Before you came to town, there was the retreat of a demoralized Polish Army. They and the local hoodlums looted our store and our house."

He had been looking at me, exhaling the smoke of his cigarette and watching the smoke rise as it formed rings and dissolved in the air. "Is that all?"

"Not yet, if you please. As I told you, a little merchandise remains in the home of our Gentile friend. It's very little, too little to be of any use to the German Army, but it means a lot to us. It could become the foundation of a new beginning after the war is over. I risked my life shopping for it in Lvov. Perhaps you could let us keep it?"

The German went slowly to the table, extinguished his cigarette butt in an ashtray and said in a soft conspiratorial voice: "I would like to help you. I am not anti-Semitic, but my colleague outside is. It's he who engineered the whole thing." He paused. "You know what, I am going to help you. Listen to me..." He went on in a hushed manner. "We will join the others now and you change your story—that because of the looting you have no yard goods at all."

"What if your colleague finds out? What will happen to me, a proven liar?"

"You do as I tell you and leave the rest to me." Energetically he opened the door and said: "The girl says they have no textiles," and went straight to the exit.

The thin German's swearing was heard long after he had slammed the door shut.

Surprised, Abner and Blume asked what I had said to bring about this turn of events.

"The truth," I said. "Perhaps I dramatized a little, but I think it was not my doing at all. The fat German just happened to be a decent human being. The thin one was the instigator of the whole thing."

"In my book they're all the same," Abner said. "It's our luck that you struck him in a special way. Let's go home, now. We've had enough for one day."

After this incident I was treated by all in the hut as if I were a celebrity. Even Father tried to overcome his penchant for silence. He pulled up one of the chairs, insisted I have a glass of tea with him and told me that he was alarmed. He felt that the Germans had him marked. That even the beggar's hut was no longer a retreat for him. He wanted to leave Niemirov, but he did not know where to go. Known to Niemirovers, he was also afraid to be caught leaving. Thus, since he had to stay on, he would feel better if I were with him.

Mark refused to move to the hut. My argument, that I spent so much time at Father's it would really make no difference if we lived there, had no effect on him. I tried to convince him how much easier it would be for me not to have to cook and not to have to run back and forth. It would save me worry about Father when I was at home and, when at Father's, concern about him and Bruno.

He would not budge.

I hinted I would move anyway. He warned me that if I did he would move too and certainly not with me. He would go to *his* parents, to Zloczov. They also needed help, he claimed.

Did he mean it? There was a great difference between our fathers. His had assimilated completely, was worldly wise, had had a higher position in a government office, spoke Polish fluently, without a trace of an accent. He spoke German also.

My father was at the other extreme. For him, the only purpose in life was to fill his mind with knowledge of the Talmud. He relinquished this task only at such times when he had to earn a living for his family. He had not been trained for that work at all. He had simply grown into it when he had inherited a flourishing business which would have probably continued to expand with or without his management. To him, no other law than the law of the Torah existed. His exterior alone gave him away for what he was.

Torn between my desire to give Father the little protection he believed I could give him and the wish not to antagonize my husband, I decided in the end that my place was with my husband.

# 20

*Where there are no men
try to be a man.*

*Sayings of the Fathers 2:6*

Bruno was sitting in his tin bathtub submerged to his chest in warm water. I coaxed him and he finally agreed to take away his hand covering the mole on his left shoulder. His appetite had improved, but he was still a thin and fragile child. I could count his ribs. He hit the surface of the water with open palms, splashing it and screaming with delight each time I pretended I was going to strike him. We laughed together and jestingly I called, "Help! Help!"

As if in answer to that call, the door opened and Blume came in. She was greatly agitated, incoherent in her efforts to tell me something.

All I could make out was that Father was in trouble. He was being beaten by Germans. At once I was at the door. "Where?" I asked.

I heard Blume's voice calling after me as I ran down the stairs, "In front of his house!"

Outside, a court official's startled glance made me aware that I probably looked awkward in the water-soaked apron, my hair wet and disheveled, and holding a cake of soap in my hand. Without stopping I put the soap in my apron pocket. Both hands free now, I unknotted the strings in the back of my waist and slipped the loop over my head. With the apron clutched under my arm I came near a curious, gaping crowd consisting of Poles and Ukrainians gathered in front of Father's house. I pushed my way through.

Father was dancing to the drums of a German soldier. He kicked up one foot, then clumsily the other, spread his arms to balance himself and someone called in German: "You dance like an elephant. Can't you hear the beat?"

His black hat and velvet skullcap he wore beneath it, fell to the ground. He jerked both of his hands to cover his dark hair in accordance with the Orthodox rule forbidding him to leave his head uncovered. His long *beckishe* (black coat made of silk) unbuttoned, the ends started to whirl as he circled. The kerchief which had covered the sides of his face slipped down around his neck. He had worn this kerchief from the day the enemy cut off one sidelock and parts of his beard. He never trimmed his beard nor did he cut off the other sidelock, also in keeping with the Orthodox law. Perspiration nestling in the remnants of his reddish beard gleamed in the sun. His face was turned upward.

The drummer kicked him in the shins and Father staggered. The same drummer caught hold of one end of his *beckishe*, pulled on it to make him come closer and ordered him to kneel. For the first time, Father resisted. It was a sin to kneel. But soon he was forced into that position anyway and drumsticks pounded rhythmically down on Father's skull.

He toppled to the ground.

He made a dazed attempt to rise but another blow and he passed out.

The crowd laughed.

Who were these people witnessing Father's shame? Yesterday, they had appeared to be his friends, today they were amused by the spectacle of his humiliation. I was not surprised at the laughter of Koreluk. He had bought textiles on the installment plan and had not made more than the first payment. When reminded, he always had the same answer: "Mr. Brand, you are rich enough, you can wait." I was not surprised at the laughter of Strzelak who had been refused credit. But what was Winnicki doing here? Why did he take pleasure in Father's fall? He who had repeatedly claimed that Mr. Brand was different from all other Jews "An honest Jew, a good man," he used to say. Did he say it only as long as he benefitted economically by Father's friendship? He mediated and profited from deals between Father buying and his client selling quarries. And there was the same court official who only a few minutes ago had crossed my path in the opposite direction, proof that news in Niemirov traveled fast. He who considered himself a member of the *intelligentsia*—why was he back here among this crowd?

When the drummer again lifted his arm to let the drumsticks down on Father's skull once more, I heard myself shout: "Stop it! Stop it!"

Automatically I pushed forward, between the court official and Winnicki. Father jerked his body as if my voice had become a source of new strength in him. He opened his eyes and looked at me. I saw a glimmer of hope in them and at that moment I would gladly have traded my life for his.

I faced the drummer. Staring steadily at his fair complexioned face, I begged: "Hit me! Please, hit me!"

He slowly turned to his buddy and asked: "What are we going to do with her?"

"We don't hit helpless women," his buddy said.

"This old man is far more helpless than I! Leave my father alone, please!"

The drummer's buddy shifted uneasily from one foot to the other. "He's all yours," he said.

"Sure, he's all yours," the drummer repeated. "You can keep him."

Both of them walked away.

Then I turned my anger on the curious. "You have no shame staying here to watch such ugliness? Some day you may regret having seen it!"

The court official scratched his head and turned to leave, Winnicki was next, and then Koreluk's chuckling died down as he also pulled away.

I stooped, caught Father under his arms and pulled him to his feet. My right shoulder fit into father's left armpit; his left arm thrown over my shoulders, we started toward his house. Together we stumbled through the rest of the dispersing spectators. His weight taxing me, the process of moving forward thirteen feet in all stretched ahead like an unconquerable mountain. I paused for a rest, but the oppressive burden did not diminish. I looked around for help. There was none to be obtained. The Gentiles had disappeared and the Jews dared not come out.

The face of *Reb* Alter appeared in the window of our next-door neighbor, the grocery store owner, but the sight was so fleeting, I was not sure I had really seen it.

Father's remark, "It must be hard on you," mobilized all my strength. I was able to reassure him, "It's not so bad. We'll soon be there."

Suddenly, two arms stronger than mine supported Father and eased my burden. It was *Reb* Alter. Never before had I welcomed anyone so heartily.

Inside, Father slumped into the first chair we reached. His face was swelling rapidly; from a cut on his forehead drops of blood were trickling in the groove between his nose and cheek, as if he had been crying red tears.

By coincidence my wet apron was still clutched under and around my arm. Now it served as first aid. I fetched water from the kitchen and washed the bruises on his face, head, and legs. In lieu of iodine, I applied vodka. Since three soldiers had held us up we kept vodka in the house as well as in the beggar's hut. Father gasped each time the alcohol-soaked apron touched a sore spot. I found a towel to apply cold compresses to his forehead and with that my knowledge of first aid was exhausted.

"Now tell me, *Reb* Lejzor, why did you have to leave the beggar's hut?" *Reb* Alter asked.

"I had to. I didn't take along the Zohar (Book of Splendor) and also wanted to check a commentary of Maimonides. I couldn't find these volumes among the books we had brought to the hut. No one was around to send for the right ones. I had almost reached the house when those hoodlums caught me." He moved up in the chair, seeking a more comfortable position and an expression of pain passed over his face.

Despite my understanding that studying for my father was more important than food, I was annoyed. A sharp remark that he be more restrained was on my tongue, but *Reb* Alter's agreeable nodding of his head made me maintain silence.

"Does it hurt?" I asked.

"Not too much. It probably looks worse than it is."

"I'll take him to the hut," *Reb* Alter volunteered.

"Perhaps I can make it on my own," Father said.

"Perhaps you can, but I am going to take you home."

"Are you coming along, Roma?" Father asked. There was an element of pleading in his voice. Under the swollen lids, his eyes probed me as he was waiting for my answer.

Thinking of Mark, I hesitated. After a moment I said:

"Sure, I'm coming along and I'm going to stay with you, Father."

"So what are we waiting for, let's go!" His voice had changed, he sounded as if the pain had left him.

Perele started to cry when *Reb* Alter brought Father into the hut. Asking no questions, she immediately took charge of nursing him back to health.

I sent Abner with a note to Mark:

> Dearest:
> Father was beaten badly. I am going to stay with him overnight and expect you and Bruno to join me before curfew. I trust you will understand.
> Love.

Then I waited.

Would Mark come and stay in a poor hut among beggars and Hasidim whom he detested, or would he refuse this time, too, as he had many times before? Suppose he didn't come? I had to do what I did for Father's sake and also for my own.

I looked longingly at the entrance door expecting Abner's return with an answer.

At last it opened and in came Bruno, rushing into my arms. "Mummy, I love you," he said.

"I love you too, my little bird, more than anybody in the wide world." And when Abner entered followed by Mark I let go of Bruno and grasped Mark's hand and pressed it to my cheek. "Thank you, my dear, thank you."

It was more than gratitude I wanted to express. Now I could think that Mark, despite his stern and rigid behavior, was essentially a kind and sympathetic person and I also took pride in having made my own decision.

That night, Perele served dinner in two shifts for the eighteen people now comprising the beggar's "family." All we had was a kind of thick soup consisting of diced potatoes and beans, a slice of bread and tea. The small kerosene lamp cast a wavering shadow over the rough surface of the table, barely reaching my father who rested in a broken wicker chair in a corner of the room. From time to time I heard him sigh.

A sharp knock at the entrance door, and we froze. All of us knew that only Germans would dare be on the streets at this time of the evening.

Somehow it became my responsibility to open the door. With sign language I motioned the men to hide in the lean-to, where firewood was stacked. They moved on tiptoe and locked themselves from inside. I pulled worn blankets over Father so that now he seemed a pile of dirty laundry that had been tossed in a corner.

Only then did I open the entrance door.

A lone German in uniform stood outside and asked, in a voice that bore little resemblance to the usual commanding shouts we had become accustomed to, if he might come in. When he stepped into the range of the light, I recognized the heavy-set soldier who only a few days ago had made it possible for us to keep our yard goods.

He put a package on the table. "I am sure you can make good use of the food I brought for you. Yes," he emphasized after his glance brushed the table, "I am sure."

I shook off my surprise and asked: "How did you find us here?"

"That was no problem. I saw you today. You know, if medals were given for defying evil, you would surely receive one. But those days have passed." He paused as if weighing his words, "*Fraulein*," he went one, "don't ever again let your emotions get the upper hand. You got away with it once. It was a miracle. Next time, no miracle. You don't know our *goldene Jugend* (golden youth). May I sit down?"

Astonished by his remarks I did not know what to make of them. However, when he began unpacking bread, sardines and chocolate and suggested we finish dinner with the addition of these delicacies, I preferred to believe that his intentions were good or, at least, harmless.

Not so the rest of us. But since by tacit agreement I was to open the door, the first to face the enemy, to be the speaker for all, plainly the representative for the eighteen members of the unit living in the beggar's hut, I grew quickly into that role. I coaxed those at the table to resume eating.

Also the German encouraged us to eat.

The first one was the beggar's wife. With a knife she attacked one of the three sardines cramped in the upper row of the can. She shared one sardine with her two daughters. Perele divided another between me and Blume.

While we were eating, the German watched us indulgently as many people do when they watch children eat. Then he took Tin-Tin on his lap and said: "Poor creature, I'll have some milk for you tomorrow."

Skinny Tin-Tin meowed, broke loose and ran to Perele.

The German took out of his pocket a bottle of vodka and poured a little into each of our tea glasses, perplexed about how many there were. He picked up the one I had rinsed for him, raised it, looked over his shoulder and said in a low voice: "To Hitler's downfall."

I wondered whether my sense of hearing was deluding me and quickly exchanged a frightened glance with Blume. Her shocked face convinced me that she had heard the same thing.

The German, glass in hand, looked at me as if perceiving that I had been elected to represent all gathered in that room: "Tell them that I mean it," he said. "I detest *him* more than your people do."

We kept quiet.

"My father and brother are rotting in a concentration camp for no reason at all. I wish Hitler dead. And I know your wish is the same after what the two boorish youths did to your father. I also know that our mutual wish shall come true sooner than you think. Please, trust me, drink!" He banged his glass against mine, "To his death," he said and gulped his vodka in one swallow. "Please, don't be afraid of me."

My last doubt had dissolved. I took a sip of vodka and so did Blume and the beggar's wife. I asked Perele in Polish to fetch the men from the lean-to.

"Do you really think it's all right?" she asked.

"Don't you?"

Obediently she went to the back door, tapped twice, paused and tapped three times and again twice. Upon this familiar code knock, the door was unbolted from inside and first Abner appeared on the threshold. Noticing the German, he was shocked and quickly retreated, but Father, who had heard the German speak, had thrown back some of the blankets and encouraged Abner in Yiddish to enter.

The German looked flabbergasted at Father in the corner, at Abner, at the few men following Abner, and then he laughed heartily. "You have nothing to be afraid of," he said.

Mark murmured something under his breath about my being crazy, exposing him to the mercy of a German.

"This is a *friend*, Mark, and this is my husband," I said.

The German coaxed the men to drink: "To the death of the *Fuhrer!*"

Abner paled. Mark nudged my arm. The beggar, not understanding the German language, took a generous bite from the open sandwich his wife had prepared for him. When asked to drink, he hurriedly swallowed the bread thinly spread with the oil of the sardines. He licked his fingers and said that *this* German was a good German.

Soon the German had Abner engaged in a political discussion. Abner strongly disagreed with the German's claim that Hitler had already lost the war. "Hitler's troops are marching forward meeting little or no resistance at all. Taking this part of Poland, all farm country, he assured himself of a sufficient supply of food, the most important factor in the war."

"You are mistaken if you think that Hitler's move into Poland was a smart one. This is one step more toward his disaster. It's only a question of time and time is running out for him. Just picture an elastic. Stretch it. Stretch it a little more. Each expansion weakens the band; give it another pull and it snaps. Hitler has an army. It's a big army. It's a powerful one. But with each territory he occupies he must leave a part of that army behind to hold the conquered territory. Every victory means stretching the elastic more tautly. His house painter's mind doesn't know that an elastic also has a breaking point."

Mark repeatedly nudged my knee under the table not to say anything.

"Hitler has no human emotions," the German went on when he realized that nobody dared to speak up. "He was wounded during the First World War and he lost all sexual desires. He has no wife, no children and I personally believe he has a splinter in his brain." He tapped his index-finger against his temple. Mark whispered in Polish that all this was a trap.

So many questions burned in my mind, I nevertheless kept quiet and swallowed my vexation in an attempt to keep Mark agreeable to staying in the beggar's hut another few days.

"I have news for you. After we leave, this territory will be occupied by the Russians."

Abner's head jerked in surprise. "Is it true?" he asked.

"It is true. It's official. Hitler and Stalin reached an agreement in which Poland is to be divided between Germany and Russia and the demarcation line is going to be the rivers Oder and Neisse. Niemirov falls into the territory which will belong to the Soviets. Those units of the German Army who have advanced beyond the agreed upon demarcation line must retreat."

"Then we are in for more trouble," Abner said.

"You should be happy about this turn of events." The German turned to me. "Under a lasting German occupation your troubles would greatly increase. I myself would rather remain here. If it were not for my wife and children back home...."

Lost in my thoughts I heard only a word here, a sentence there. I missed the exchange of opinions that followed between the German and Abner.

It was late when the German left.

We never saw him again.

He had hardly closed the door when Mark pleaded caution against the strange visitor. "We should not have taken part in any criticism of Hitler and his regime. There is no doubt in my mind that this soldier is a provocateur."

Father reminded him that had he wanted to harm us, he could have done so without provoking us.

Abner said, "He is a Communist and that's why he likes Stalin more than Hitler. Don't worry, Mark, he's not going to harm us."

Our bickering continued late into the night.

# 21

*The mind of each man is as unique
as his face.*

Adapted from Talmud, Berakoth, 58a

Father calling my name from the adjoining room woke me up at six in the morning. I slipped quietly out of bed so as not to disturb Mark and threw a houserobe over my shoulders. In the first room, Father was sitting upright whispering: "Someone is knocking at the door."

New trouble? Pushing my arms through the sleeves of my robe, I asked "Who is it?"

"It's me, Trusievicz," the familiar voice of our Gentile friend answered.

I removed the chain from the loop. Inside, Ivan said in a voice almost too low to hear: "They sentenced seven Jews to death last night—your father among them. If he can hide within the next four hours, he may be able to save himself. Not a word to anyone!" He pressed my arm until it hurt and kept on pleading, "I beg of you, not a living soul must know that I was here!"

"Please, tell me, why was Father sentenced to death?"

"Wasn't Hirschfeld shot? Your father was also an active member of the town administration before they took over."

"Who are the other six? They have to be alerted too," Father said.

"I'm running to Lefkovicz, to Weniger, and to Schall. Look outside. See if the way is clear."

He could lose his job with the German town administration, I realized, if it became known that he had not ended his friendly relationship with Jews. And now had risked his life to warn us. I stuck my head out and seeing nobody I nodded to Ivan that it was safe to leave.

Father started to dress. He moaned when he reached for his trousers. But there was no time for sympathy. "Make it snappy," I said and went to the other room, tapped Mark's shoulder and apologized for waking him to go and see Father. Then I ran to the barn and fetched Abner. Everyone gathered in Father's room and everybody had a different suggestion about what to do.

The final decision was that Father dress in beggar's clothing and that the beggar himself would accompany Father to the village of Radroz, where we knew a few peasants. Perhaps one of them would be willing to take him in. He had in mind Stefan Szwirk who had been a part-time employee, paid in advance by Father many times to ward off one or another emergency. In the past Stefan Szwirk had left his fields whenever a deadline on the road construction had to be met. Over the years a friendship had developed which Father was now to put to the test.

"Will you be able to walk all the way to Radroz?" Abner asked.

"Don't worry, I'll make it all right."

Abner went into the kitchen, now the landlord's bedroom. In a minute or so he was back to tell us that the landlord agreed. We discussed how we would ever know whether the two men had reached Radroz safely.

It was decided that Blume and I were to follow, keeping within a watchful distance of the two beggars. We were, according to Abner's plans, to carry knapsacks strapped to our shoulders. If questioned, we would say that we were repatriates on our way to Cracow.

I woke Blume, advised her to dress quickly, to put on comfortable shoes and promised to explain everything later. Perele had already prepared two knapsacks stuffed with bulky sweaters which weighed little and filled the knapsacks.

Meanwhile, Father had dressed in what he had borrowed from his landlord. Despite the grave situation, I could not keep from laughing when I saw the finished creation of that masquerade. He wore black trousers with two blue and white striped patches on the knees. Much too long, they were rolled up at the ankles. A shirt, probably once white but now of undetermined color, was frayed at the collar and along the front with all but one button missing. A much too large, richly stained lightweight coat had navy-blue patches at the elbows. The sleeves, rolled up, exposed the torn lining. Only the white kerchief, wound around his face and knotted on top of his head as if he was suffering from a toothache, contrasted sharply with the rest of his appearance.

The beggar's wife suggested replacing it and now one more color, green, adorned my father. A plain rope around his waist supported the phylacteries hidden behind the coat. Advised by the beggar to leave the phylacteries home, Father flatly refused.

"How will I say my morning prayers?" he asked with indignation.

Over his back, the beggar threw a burlap sack containing yard goods which he would try to exchange for flour, butter, chickens and eggs in Radroz. He seemed unperturbed about the risk he was taking by this escape. Since our food supply was nearly used up, he had planned it anyway, he said.

We started out on the highway, turned off at a dirt road and then to a small path leading into the woods. The beggar walked briskly and Father kept his pace well ahead of us. The notion came to me again that Father must derive the spiritual and physical strength he manifested in meeting these calamities head on from some mysterious source. He hadn't raised his voice during the preparations; not once had he complained of his pain which surely had not disappeared overnight. What power sustained him? He submitted to this distasteful masquerade with detachment; he kissed the doorpost *mezuza* on his way out of the house and made a cheerful remark to his wife: "So God willing, I'll be back soon."

"Father seems much better today," Blume said.

"Father is an extraordinary human being," I said and urged her to hasten as the distance between us and the two "beggars" began to widen.

I became aware that we had seen no Germans since we left the highway. They seemed to be staying close to the main arteries.

We saw Father safely installed in Stefan Szwirk's shanty. The real beggar stayed long enough to shop for food while Blume and I went back unmolested and were much more at ease knowing Father was out of Niemirov and beyond reach of our enemy.

# 22

*If we don't help someone in need,
it is as if we ourselves are the cause of his need.*

Hasidic saying

Bruno played happily in the beggar's hut as he had played in his own or grandfather's more comfortable homes. Often he acted as if he were a daddy to little Lisa; he acted as if he were a dentist when an adult pretended to have a toothache and he ran from the hut to the barn and back a hundred times. Sometimes he hid in the lean-to and acted deaf to our calls, just as Mark, Father, and Abner did when they were afraid to be caught by the enemy.

His playfulness became a source of irritation to Mark. "He can learn nothing but bad manners here. Can't you see what's becoming of our child? You asked me and I agreed to come over for *one* night. Five have passed. Enough is enough. We're going home," he said, while Bruno had once more hidden in the lean-to.

I went inside and found Bruno behind a barrel filled with pickles. His cheeks rosy from excitment, he laughed heartily, convinced I would never have found him had he not voluntarily revealed his presence.

I could see no harm in these childish pranks nor could I detect any change for the worse in his behavior. But I held back in response to Mark's derisive and insulting remarks and hoped that Abner, Blume, and Perele who must have overheard them would keep quiet too. The child who had never had so many people around him, enjoyed it. The inconveniences for us—the lack of privacy or waiting for the outhouse to be vacant—were adventures to Bruno.

Sometimes Abner and Sara gave me a quick, significant glance. I liked nothing better than to signal in return that I, too, was in disagreement with a statement Mark proclaimed but, to avoid a quarrel between me and my husband, I restrained myself. I was grateful to them for pretending not to notice his snobbery. One and all tried to please Mark in an attempt to have us stay with them. That's why they considered his wishes, his comforts first and always.

"Please, Mark, bear with it a little longer," I pleaded. "I will make it up to you somehow, please?"

"Why, you're more concerned with their well-being than with your son's!"

"Bruno will be all right. Anyway, I promise, I will double my efforts after the war is over."

"I'll never stay with them that long."

"I didn't mean it that way. I meant to say that Bruno and you shall be the only ones to receive my attention and affection; all right Mark? But right now my relatives are desperate for our help."

"Why are they so important to you?"

"Isn't your family to you? Come on now, let's have lunch. We have corn-on-the-cob today and you and Bruno like it so much."

Shouts to open up and pounding on the door prevented Mark from answering me. He disappeared momentarily in the lean-to and I called Abner from the other room to follow him. Then I opened the front door.

Two Germans in uniform and one Ukrainian had come for Lejzor Brand.

"Mr. Brand is not here," I said.

They ransacked the attic, the cellar and the lean-to. They made Mark and Abner come out. One German, addressed by the other as Kurt, asked them what their relationship was to Lejzor Brand and upon learning that one was the son and the other the son-in-law, they ordered them to come along. Mark, slow in complying with the order was shouted at: "Are you hard of hearing? *Judenschwein!* Otto, kick him out."

Mark quickly moved on and I followed close behind them,

wondering whether Mark and Abner were being taken according to Ivan's information, instead of Father.

Kurt whispered something into the Ukrainian's ear. The Ukrainian departed and disappeared into the first house we passed and after a short while he reappeared carrying an empty pail. Kurt took it from him and turning to Mark shouted an order: "Fill it up. We need water. Go to that pump and fill it up!"

The pump was about twenty feet away. I understood very well how humiliated Mark must have felt so I followed him to help him pump the water.

Kurt called: "Hey you! You stay here."

Soon Mark returned, carrying the water-filled pail by the handle with both hands. The water splashed around with every step he made. Both Kurt and Otto screamed with laughter while a few Gentile onlookers gathered. Kurt pointed at Mark: "This clumsy ox can't even carry a bucket of water properly."

"I am an attorney, not a..."

"There are no longer Jewish attorneys. You are a swine, that's what you are!" Kurt took the water-filled pail from Mark, hoisted it high up and, swinging the pail over Mark's head, poured the water over him.

Mark shivered.

I shivered.

The onlookers laughed.

I pleaded with Kurt to leave my husband alone. In response he roared: "Have a better look at this little dish. She claims to be the wife of the clumsy fool who calls himself a man. Not bad, eh?" Turning back to Mark, he snapped: "All right, Jew, you can go. He's not worth bothering with anyway."

Water dripping from him, his clothing clinging to his body, his gold-rimmed glasses in his hand, Mark scurried away. When I started after him, Kurt stopped me: "Not you. You stay here."

Kurt shoved me and Otto shoved Abner toward the pump.

I could sense their effort to invent a scheme that would entertain both themselves and the growing number of the curious. Kurt again whispered something into the ear of the Ukrainian. The Ukrainian took the pail, went into the first house, returned with it and handed it to me.

"Fill it up." Kurt said.

Nothing easier, I thought. I placed the pail under the faucet and pumped. At first, the water came slowly. Then in a swift stream. But the pail did not fill. Kurt laughed, his blue eyes sparkling with delight for his clever joke worked perfectly. He had punched holes in the bottom of the pail. Tossing his blond hair back, he stopped laughing and hollered: "I will slowly count to ten and if the bucket is not filled your laziness will be punished. Remember, the bucket better be full!"

It was Abner who had to take the punishment for my "laziness." He was punched in the abdomen and kicked to the ground. With his groans in my ears, I bent to my task with more vigor. I pumped faster, faster, faster. It became a speed marathon that would perhaps buy the life of my brother. The life he must give instead of Father.

The pumping went on endlessly. I pumped like an automaton, as if this function had always been part of my life. Then I slipped and fell.

One thought penetrated through the haziness of my mind: I must get up to go on pumping, get up! Get up! Some new strength came to me when I thought there was none. I could reach for the iron and wanted to use it as support to get up, but I cut my hand on a sharp edge and I slipped to nothingness.

I was probably out for seconds because next I felt someone grabbing my arm and dragging me directly under the faucet. "I'll give that dirty Jew a bath right here," I heard Kurt's voice. Cold water streamed over me and revived me. Through my eyelashes I saw Kurt's blue eyes and they seemed to express a trace of sympathy as he looked down at me and my bleeding hand. But I was wrong. He pushed the handle down, pulled it up, pushed it down with a fury as if his life depended on it. No longer sensitive to that waterfall, I tried to catch my breath and then I heard Otto's voice over the noise made by the joined metals.

"Let's go, Kurt. These two are finished."

"But *I* haven't finished yet."

I kept pretending that I had not regained consciousness, opened my eyes only slightly and saw them leave.

Bent with pain, Abner had to make his way to the hut on his own. I could not help him. My strength was gone.

Though he was later lying in the same corner Father had recently vacated, I felt that mercy had been granted us for we expected that the Germans had come to take Abner's and Mark's life for Father's

Sara lovingly attended Abner's broken ribs and bruises. With Lisa in her arms, she crossed the tiny room many times passing me without as much as a glance. She still held a grudge for my having summoned her husband to face the Germans who wanted our textiles. On rare occasions when I was able to catch her eyes they were full of reproach. Even Lisa broke loose from my arms.

Perele helped me out of my clothes, bandaged my hand and I slipped into bed. Resting under the covers, I asked: "Where is Mark?"

Instead of fetching him, my stepmother sat down on the edge of my bed. Her black almond-shaped eyes looked at me sympathetically. "Mark came home as wet as you did. He changed his clothes and left for your apartment. He told me how humiliated he felt and said he would never again be able to face the people in this town. He wouldn't let me squeeze in a word edgewise. I doubt whether he was fully aware of what he said."

I jumped out of bed, yanked out another dress from the broken wooden closet and hurried to our apartment.

Mark was not there.

From the apartment I went to his office which had been closed since the day the war had started. Neither was he there. I knew his exaggerated sense of pride and what a terrible blow it must have been for him to be ridiculed and laughed at by the same people who only a few weeks back had taken off their hats whenever they crossed his path. But weren't we living in extraordinary times? Wasn't everything accepted and acceptable so long as one could remain alive?

I sat down on a chair, thick with dust. The office had a musty, unused odor. I bent my head over the desk and wept.

So immersed was I in my own misery that I did not hear Blume enter the office until she was almost upon me. She handed me a letter. It read:

"My dearest Roma:
My love for you and our son is boundless.
In spite of it, my life in Niemirov is no longer worth

living. Since your attachment to your family will not permit you to leave them, I am compelled to leave you with them. I am going to Zloczov to stay with my parents. I hope you will take good care of our son, at least as good as you took of your father. We will be together as a family as soon as circumstances permit. I hope it will be soon..."

# 23

*He who prays for his neighbor
will be heard for himself.*

Talmud: Baba Kama, 92b

The beggar did not want us to stay any longer for his hut had been marked by the Germans. Our Christian friend, Ivan Trusievicz, also advised us to move out for the same reason.

A Mrs. Dvojre Letzter, living on the outskirts of town, offered to take us in. The beggar's family, *Reb* Alter and Benny's mother carried our personal belongings in small bundles to her house.

At dawn, before curfew, in order not to arouse anyone's attention, each of us went separately through different streets to our new home. Here, all of us slept on the floor on stacks of hay, except Perele, for whom Dvojre Letzter's only daughter, Jula, gave up her bed.

Bruno and Lisa enjoyed it all. The secrecy, the moving, the new surroundings and especially the garden in the back of the house. Once "settled," the adults, having little to do when not at compulsory jobs, gave the two children their undivided attention.

Abner made steady improvement and Stefan Szwirk's neighbor from Radroz stopped by to tell us that Father was in good health and spirits. Except for Mark's absence our family was alive and well.

The steady stream of German troops passing Niemirov on

their way back westward gave evidence that the heavy-set German had been accurately informed. It looked like a planned retreat.

It was after lunch, the dishes washed and put away. I had the rare pleasure of being all alone with Bruno in the kitchen. He had ceased to play; he was dozing in my lap. My child's warmth, his regular breathing, the quiet in the house affected my own state of mind. I stopped reproaching myself for Mark's absence and, hoping he had reached Zloczov safely, I regretted nothing. Some still wakeful part of me intended to go to the barn with Bruno and nap comfortably on the hay but I was too lazy to do it. My face dropped and rested upon Bruno's head. His silken hair exuded the scent of freshly cut hay.

Several excited voices outside claimed my full awareness. Soon, friends of my father's burst into the kitchen awakening Bruno with their wailing, "The synagogue, the synagogue!" *Reb* Alter among them, his face half covered by his grayish curly beard, only inches away from me, said, "Roma, you must help!" For the first time he called me by my name.

In the noise and confusion which drowned out some of *Reb* Alter's words, I understood that the group of about fifteen Jews had just come from the synagogue where German soldiers were desecrating the place of worship. The sexton and his son bravely asked the soldiers to stop but were beaten up. The soldiers boasted that they were going to pour gallons of kerosene over everything and toss a match into the synagogue the next morning, burning the temple to the ground and lighting their way out of town.

"What has all this to do with me?"

In answer to my question *Reb* Alter said: "We have a plan. You will go to their Commander and ask him for protection. You will convince him as you convinced the other German before. You will tell him that we are willing to part with our last *groszen*, with our silver and jewels, only let them not destroy our *shul*."

Immediately everyone present pledged something or other.

"Quiet!" *Reb* Alter urged. "One can't hear one's own voice! You see," he said to me, "you could tell the Commander that a ransom of gold and silver is to their advantage, burning the *shul* is not."

Remembering the advice given me by the heavy-set German to mind my own business, I replied that I could not go to the Commander. It would be walking into a lion's den and I had a child to take care of.

"You're the only one, you must go!" The words sounded more like an order than a plea.

The lament increased and Bruno started to cry. Dvojre Letzter took the child from me and led him out of the house to the garden.

"*Reb* Alter, I can't do it. Besides, my going would be of no help."

"You mean you refuse to even try?" *Reb* Alter said with indignation. "You wouldn't refuse if your father were here and asked you. You know something? The Rabbi himself wanted to leave his hiding place and come to ask you personally to go but I didn't let him."

"All right. All right, I'll go, whatever that means. But I promise nothing else. I'll go to the synagogue to see for myself what this is all about."

Near the synagogue, women with children in their arms, men with bundles on their backs were hurrying here and there; the whole vicinity was in an uproar. The German threat had spread speedily and all local inhabitants were moving to other parts of the town.

The group which had started out from Dvojre Letzter's house became smaller on the way to the synagogue. By the time I entered the house of worship, only *Reb* Alter and Benny's mother were with me.

I had seldom been there. I usually went on the Day of Atonement to say a prayer for my deceased mother. On those days the synagogue was filled to capacity, with the men downstairs and the women in the balcony. Through the tiny glass windows I could imagine seeing my father wrapped in his *tallith* trimmed with gold braids, standing by the lectern. His eyelids closed most of the time, he moved the upper part of his body from side to side or rocked back and forth rhythmically as he sang either the sad or the jubilant prayers in a clear baritone voice. The worshippers, men downstairs, women in the balcony, answered in chorus. My father, strikingly handsome, his arms outstretched to emphasize a more dramatic verse, his deep-blue eyes sometimes turning upward, glowing mystically and detached, was himself a symbol of peace and holiness.

Now a different picture unfolded: The grotesque figure of a dancing Jew, performing a pitiful bizarre rendition of the whirling dervish for the amusement of German soldiers. I saw him bending, bowing, twisting and jumping at the command of two hooligans in uniform. I saw him beaten, I heard his shrieks and I saw him fall. I saw one of the two step on the hem of his floor-length coat when he was about to get up. The Jew lay in the gutter, unmoving, a beaten man.

Would he ever rise?

*Father, you must rise, you must stand erect again! I will do everything in my power for you to have your prayer house intact and I promise that if I don't succeed I will build a temple for you, the just one . . .*

"For the sake of your Father, you must go to the Commander," I heard *Reb* Alter say.

"Where am I to find this Commander?"

He did not know, nor did I expect he would.

Outside, Jews had gathered again. They looked at us with admiration for having the courage to enter a place marked as a target by the Germans. "Is she going?" one and another asked as if everything depended on my decision to go. Benny's mother was among them and she offered the information that part of the General Staff directing the retreat to the River San was set up in the house of the town's druggist.

Benny's mother and six other Jews started out with me in the direction of Rava-Ruska Street and, as before, drifted away as we came closer to the house of the druggist.

The druggist said it was foolish even to try, but when I insisted, he showed me to the door. I knocked and after a man's voice called, "*Herein,*" I entered.

The man in uniform, bent over a large map on his desk, without turning his head to the entrance, asked: "What do you want?"

"I came here—"

Surprised, he faced me.

Ignorant of his military rank, I could not decide how to address him. I busied myself with adjusting my blue babushka and said: "Please *Herr Offizier*, we need your help. Your soldiers are in the process of destroying a J—" swallowing the word Jewish, I went on, "—place of worship. They threaten to burn it to the ground."

"It's a synagogue, isn't it?"

I nodded.

"And you want *me* to help you save a Jewish place of worship? You're out of your mind!"

"I don't care so much about the synagogue," I stuttered, "but—many Gentiles lived there. The poorest of the town live in—in this neighborhood and all of them will suffer alike."

"Go to the proper authorities," he said and stepped up to me and shoved me out of the room.

"Where can I find the proper authorities?" I asked as he shut the door in front of my nose.

"Try the notary's house."

Benny's mother, her frail body leaning against the outside wall, was waiting for me. She told me that *Reb* Alter had made her promise to look after me. He himself had to leave for the *Minche-Maariv* prayers he would not miss. The absence of *Reb* Alter deflated my courage. In another half hour it would be curfew and I would have to explain my being outside if I were seen by the patrolling Germans.

But I set out in a fast stride with Benny's mother trying to keep pace with me.

Two soldiers, standing guard in front of Moshe Schall's only three-story building in town, stopped us at a distance. After I called out my request to see an officer in charge, there was a short conference between the two and I alone was permitted to come closer.

One soldier went inside and returned shortly, preceded by a lieutenant. I repeated the story I had told the German staying in the home of the druggist. He motioned me to come over and then to follow him inside. He left me standing in the dimly-lit corridor while he disappeared through one of the many doors along the corridor on the ground floor.

I remembered this particular door leading to what had been the personal office of the Polish notary. I had been here once before with Abner, Anna, Adela, and Blume. It was after Mother's tragic death that we assembled in this office, to legally transfer our rights to the house Mother had left us, to our father.

I glanced at the other doors, wondering which one led to the notary's living quarters and concluded that he and his family had probably been evicted the day this German post supervising the retreat moved in.

Waiting tensely, now, I thought of Mother buried, of Father in exile, of Mark away, and of myself, a housewife only a few weeks ago attending to routine duties concerning my husband and child, striving for equality in a man's world but hardly daring to hope I would make more than the meagerest progress. The rest of the way I would leave to women of future generations.

Suddenly, responsibilities of magnitude I didn't know how to cope with had been thrust upon me.

I was scared.

I could be killed here.

Two hours ago Bruno rested in my lap, his warm body snuggled against my own. Who would take care of my baby if I were killed?

The lieutenant came back with a captain. I repeated my plea. The captain listened without a muscle twitching in his face. He led me one flight up to what I thought would be the place of my execution.

He knocked on a door, waiting for the familiar *herein*, and ushered me in. A very tall man without a jacket, stretched comfortably in an upholstered armchair, his long legs supported by another chair, listened to the captain's report. The tall man glanced at me and dismissed the captain.

Alone with me, he said: "Now *you* tell me in your own words what this is all about."

I had learned from the incident with the heavy-set German, that on an individual basis a man was able to elevate himself above the immorality of his group, so, having repeated my story to four different people, I would now change my approach. I would pretend to be a Polish Catholic.

"Colonel, something terrible is going on in town. *You* probably know nothing about it. It may destroy my respect for the Germans."

"What is going on?"

Fixing my eyes upon the pair of impeccably polished boots next to the armchair, one of my hands grasped the other tightly. I tried to sort out my thoughts; to make short, coherent sentences appealing to the German; but one word collided with another as if all of them had to be spoken at the same time. I half closed my eyes (Father, I am trying, I am trying) and tensed my hands while speaking.

"Your soldiers have demolished the inside of a Jewish church." I used the phrase Jewish church intentionally as a Pole would. "And they freely boast of their intention to burn it to the ground on their way out of Niemirov tomorrow morning. But this in itself is not important. One Jewish church more or less doesn't matter. Only that the shacks surrounding the Jewish church owned by Gentiles will go up like kindling—that is important! They are the town's poorest. Where will they go? Is the German aim to deprive these people of their ramshackle shelters?"

I inhaled. I shifted my eyes away from the boots to his face and tried to formulate my plea in one outcry. "Don't sacrifice the innocent when there is no important reason for it. Let *me* and the rest of our population retain the image of a German culture which contributed so much to the world!"

There was silence. Was it a good sign that he let me talk? That he didn't interrupt me?

He pulled himself up, called his orderly and the orderly helped him into his jacket. The colonel buttoned it with meticulous care, giving the same care to putting on his boots. "You will take me to where this alleged destruction is to take place. Is it far from here?"

"No. It's on Lubaczov Street."

Outside, he suddenly stopped: "*Himmeldonnerwetter!* I forgot my flashlight." He ordered one of the guards to get it for him.

Benny's mother was not in sight, not a living soul on the streets. It was dark and as we crossed the empty spacious Market Place, fear for my own life increased again. I was all alone with this giant of a German. With no witnesses, one shot would rid him of the problem. I tried to cover my fear by laughing aloud, perhaps too loud. "In order to speak to you face to face, I should need a stepladder," I said. Encouraged by his chuckle, I added: "I probably look like a comma alongside an exclamation point."

Now he, too, laughed and, as if confiding in me, he said: "You people think the German soldiers are the worst. You will soon have the Russians here, and with those barbarians, you will first realize the difference and then long for our return. You just wait and see."

A petroleum stench assailed our nostrils as we reached the synagogue. The colonel played the flashlight over the walls and shattered windows, and then inside, over the broken lamps and overturned benches.

I stared at the pulpit, the second time that day. I took a deep breath and made my voice sound without a trace of tremor: "You can see for yourself the soldiers mean business. One could smell the petroleum a mile away. You know what, you could place a guard here who would prevent the soldiers from carrying out their threat."

"*Mädel, sie sind wohl verrückt!* You talked like a crazy woman when you came to my office and you're still talking like one."

Since I was already accused of being crazy, I continued in a like manner: "How else will you prevent this horror?"

"Who said I wished to prevent it?"

All my hope dwindled. But I kept trying. "It would leave a favorable impression on *us* Poles if you spared *our* homes..." And my next comment was truly one from a crazy woman: "I hoped you would do it as a personal favor to me." He probably did not hear those words for the unusually tall colonel had walked away with long angry strides.

I wanted to say good night, but now he was certainly out of hearing. I grew so terrified at finding myself alone in the dark, outside after curfew, that I started to run from Lubaczov Street and did not stop until I was safely at Letzter's home.

Breathless, I slumped into a chair. Abner gave me a sharp questioning look. I shook my head from side to side.

Early in the morning, my fifteen-year-old cousin Jankiel knocked at the window. "Open up, open up!" he called.

He stormed into the house and told everyone who was awakened that four soldiers in three shifts had guarded the synagogue throughout the night. "They never stopped cursing *die Saujuden* (The Jewish swine) who were the cause of their extra duty."

Jankiel had played so many pranks on us so often that even

though he could have knowledge of this, because he lived near the synagogue, we did not take his story seriously.

However, soon the house filled with neighbors and friends and they confirmed his words.

Our landlady, Dvojre Letzter, said she was proud to have me under her roof and her daughter Jula became my ardent friend. Perele said she knew I could do it and *Reb* Alter almost touched my hand in gratitude.

I hardly heard what people were saying. I was dominated by one thought only: Father would have his prayer house, the prayer house he needed if he was ever to stand erect again.

# 24

*If you can't endure the bad,
you won't live long enough to enjoy the good.*

Talmud: Berakoth, 33b

The following day, a few poorly dressed young men walked in ankle deep mud through Rava-Ruska Street to the outskirts of Niemirov. They stopped at a newly erected arch and turned their heads up with an expression of pride and happiness.

Another young man, the only tinsmith in town, had just finished embellishing the arch with little red flags. Upon seeing his friends he scrambled down the stepladder and shouted: "They're coming! They're coming!"

He rushed into the arms of the shoemaker, better known as "Hooknose," but immediately fell back in a spasm of coughing. The others were too excited to pay attention to him. They were tossing their caps up in the air and jumping to catch them. Then they walked along the same street and disappeared in different directions to spread *their* joyous news: "They're coming!"

The first heavy tanks came rolling in from the east, from Rava-Ruska. They were making a right turn into the Market Place, the center of town.

I followed quickly in the slush. My sister Blume walking side by side said that she had had enough, that she was cold, and that she was going home. I called back that I was staying.

The Russian soldiers jumped down from their tanks.

They were immediatly surrounded by the four young men and their friends who suddenly reappeared.

The shoemaker's wife, "Mrs. Hooknose," shivering in a voluminous yellow dress gathered in at the waistline by a deep-red sash, had her arms full of red roses. She was holding them out to one of the Russians as he emerged from a tank.

The tinsmith with one little red flag sticking out of his frayed coatpocket was embracing another soldier. Others in his group vied to shake hands and say a few words of welcome to the new occupiers.

Smiling brighly, the Russians looked on, somewhat bewildered by the commotion.

It seemed strange to me that only three weeks ago the entry of the German Army had been celebrated in a similar fashion. Instead of red flags there had been a broken cross, and instead of Lenin's and Stalin's pictures, Hitler's picture. Today the Welcoming Committee consisted of poor workers representing all three denominations living in our part of Poland. Three weeks ago it had consisted only of Ukrainian nationalists. Like the Ukrainians at that time, now the poor workers were unafraid of the invaders. Having met the workers face to face in the past only when they happened to render some service, they had then impressed me as polite and timid people. Their present assertiveness more than surprised me. One of them pushed me out of his way, another shoved me aside, neither of them apologizing.

Now, in addition to the Committee, other people came out of their homes and remained standing close to the buildings, looking on with suspicion and fear as they did a few weeks ago. Some of them walked hesitantly toward the tanks and soon more followed.

Jews remained aloof. The past few weeks had been filled with too much horror; it would take some time to shake it off.

The warm laughter, the friendliness of the Russians somewhat diminished my worries, created and nourished by ugly rumors spread about the Russians.

I moved closer to my father's house, which was once again our home.

Inside, Bruno was playing with skinny Tin-Tin. He came towards me, holding in his fragile hands a book with Lenin's picture splashed over the cover. "Mummy, look what I have! A soldier gave me this and said he is the greatest man in the world."

"Let me have it," I said, trying to take the book from him.

He held on to it. "The soldier let me wear his cap, Mummy."

Then he reluctantly let go of the book, but not before I had promised to return it to him next day.

I pondered the impact the Russian had made on my impressionable son on his first day in Niemirov, and concluded that all quarrelling between me and Mark about our child's upbringing was senseless.

"It's almost bedtime, Darling."

"I don't want to go to bed. Grandma said Daddy is coming home."

"It's late, you have to go to bed."

"Will you wake me when he comes?" He looked at me with great round eyes.

"I promise."

"May I take Tin-Tin to my room?"

"You may."

He followed me upstairs with the cat in his arms. I undressed him and helped him into his pajamas. Then, as usual, we rubbed noses and I began to tell him the story of Snow White and The Seven Dwarfs and he fell asleep.

# 25

*A true Jew is distinguished by
three characteristics: sympathy,
modesty, benevolence.*

Sayings of the Fathers, 5:22

Father had lost weight eating only dry bread in the house of the peasant. Of the foods available, bread was the only item in keeping with the Jewish dietary laws. Upon entering, he kissed the doorpost *mezuzah* and said: "Thank God for that." This, his favorite expression of gratitude for all blessings large or small, prompted a quick retort from Abner.

"It isn't over yet. Now we have the Communists to deal with, not only the Russians but also the local folks."

Father's smile disappeared for a second but his words sounded confident and prophetic as well: "The Communists may cause us lots of hardship but never like the Nazis. Anyway, God's ways are not known to us mortals. May His will be our law."

Friday, late afternoon, the *shammes* again walked from house to house knocking with his wooden hammer on every door, a reminder that it was soon time to go to the synagogue for the evening prayer.

Later, Father returned from evening prayers in Sabbath attire. The hem of his black *beckishe* reached down to his ankles and there a bit of white socks showed. His trousers gathered below the knees stuck in his white socks. The twisted, braided silk sash ending in long tassels dangled from his waist. And the *shtreimel* (broad-brimmed black velvet hat trimmed with fur) quivered as he walked.

When Father wore his Sabbath attire, he was a man wrapped in the tranquility of his faith. Only when he changed back to everyday clothes would he once again be a man buffeted by the currents of his time.

Entering the house, he was followed as usual on Saturdays by two *Orchim*, actually wandering beggars. He crossed the little hallway, the living room, and headed for the dining room. There, he invited the *Orchim* to take a chair to the left and the right of his own chair at the head of the long table which was festively set. The *Orchim* hesitated to seat themselves until Father nodded reassuringly to them.

The pleasure of our reunion was clouded only for me. The *Orchim* made me think of Mark perhaps stranded in some town on the way to Zloczov. Perhaps he, too, had to accept a handout from strangers?

I busied myself placing two more settings on the white damask cloth. Father's deep-blue eyes, concerned and compassionate, were fixed upon me. "You haven't heard from Mark, have you?"

"No, I haven't," I said and forced a smile.

The six candles flickered. The silver candlesticks were the ones which had been stolen by the retreating Polish soldiers. We had bought them back from the Gentile to whom the soldier had traded them for two bottles of vodka. I wished that Father's face would again radiate happiness and serenity as it had a minute ago. Our glances met again and he said lovingly: "Even the rabbi changed his mind about you. He always thought you set a bad example to other Jewish daughters, but in saving the *shul* you redeemed yourself." And to the *Orchim* he explained: "You know, it was my daughter, this one, Roma, who saved the *shul*. Everywhere the Germans burned the *shuls* to the ground. They did so in Horyniec, in Lubaczov, but not in Niemirov, because my daughter went to the Commander himself to prevent this."

The one to the left of Father said: "I've heard about that miracle."

I myself derived quite a different satisfaction from the results of my action. No matter how my father or the *Orchim* or the townspeople phrased the happening (which actually *Reb* Alter initiated), henceforth I would be recognized for what I was. A person.

Father filled a silver goblet and said the *kiddush*. He took a sip of the wine and handed the goblet to his wife. She handed it to me, the oldest daughter present. The goblet made the customary round from the oldest to the youngest. In the same order, the men stepped to the enamel basin and recited a blessing, poured water three times over each hand. Father dried his hands and then handed the towel to the *Orchim*. Abner took the towel the *Orchim* had used.

Father said another blessing over the bread, one twisted loaf and one plain white bread covered with white cloth embroidered with the blue star of David. All of us repeated the prayers and then let our teeth sink into the fluffy texture of the home-baked bread. Since the customary appetizer of fish was not available, meatballs, seasoned, dressed and prepared like *gefilte* fish, served as substitute. They almost tasted like fish.

The *Orchim* dipped chunks of bread in the gravy and scooped the imitation fish from the plate. Father, eager to make them feel at home, also put his fork aside. So did Abner. Bruno followed their example watching with amusement how the white bread soaked up the golden colored gravy. I mused how Mark would have disapproved of this.

Father complimented his wife on the tasty chicken soup, took Bruno on his knees and curling his right sidelock, the one the Germans didn't cut, tapped his feet rhythmically as he sang *zmiros* (table hymns). Abner's tenor joined Father's baritone and, encouraged by Father, the two *Orchim* joined in.

Women were not to partake in the singing. However, on exceptional occasions Father pretended not to hear the female voices participating. This was such an occasion. My father was happy for many reasons and, to top it, he was also proud of me for the first time. Would my husband be proud of me?

The thought flashed through my mind. Of the two men my father was by far the stronger. Living by the rules and laws of the Torah he dismissed the changes the centuries had brought since Moses. He demanded little of life and expected less. Serving his God let him live in peace with himself.

Mark was as determined as Father. His goal, however, was not peace with God, but peace with the Gentiles, to be accepted by them. He repudiated everything that indicated Jewishness. In his opinion the Hasidim, the Orthodox, were the root of Gentile rejection. He tried to find a place in a world foreign to him, hoped to win the aliens over by rejecting the culture from which he had sprung. He collapsed, unable to withstand the first storm and tried to run away from circumstances which forced him to face his Jewishness. He ran away from me, the witness to the collapse of his philosophy.

Now the thought that he might need my help more than Father made me long for him.

I glanced at Bruno on his grandfather's lap and wished that Bruno would grow up to be a man who found strength in his heritage without shutting himself off from the world. I wished that he would be open to secular knowledge and technological progress, that in his life he would find a synthesis of the old and the new, and that he would belong to a generation that built bridges between Jews and Gentiles without either having to deny their roots.